DEEP GAP

JODY KAYE

Special Edition Paperback

First Print: January 2024

www.JodyKaye.com

Splinter of Hope
Shred of Decency
Sliver of Truth
Holding Onto Hope
Home Wrecker
Deep Gap
Bleeding Heart
Shattered Soul

Can two lonely hearts

find a promise for tomorrow?

Chapter One

Greer

"Let me drive you," Karen offers.

I pause, shrugging on the thin coat I bought at the donation center before the winter weather set in. The collar has gotten stuck underneath the back of the jacket and my shirt sleeves have ridden up to my elbows. I should either take it off and try again or find a mirror to un-bunch everything.

"Please, Greer. It's cold out." I hear my mom's voice in Karen's reminder and see her concern that I'm not protected from the elements.

Turning from the soulful expression that I'm still unable to handle, I decide I'll be going back to the thrift shop for a thicker coat before Karen runs to the mall to buy one for me. I've taken too much from her.

You took everything from her.

"I walked here. It's no big deal. I walk everywhere." I stop fiddling and pull up my shirt, exposing the mismatched tank top I'm wearing underneath. Another donation center find I'd worn all summer when it was sweltering in Brighton. "See layers!"

For Karen's sake, I keep it cheerful and walk toward

the front door without meeting the worrisome crinkles at the corner of her eyes. She was kind enough to feed me a huge breakfast before I go to work. I refuse to take advantage of her hospitality. The whole reason I agreed to come over was that I'd spent Thanksgiving with my mom and dad when Karen had wanted all three of us here. I hate disappointing her.

When I glance into the mirror there, my own face betrays the act I'm putting on for Karen's benefit. I don't recognize the detached woman who is staring back at me with her stringy blonde hair secured in a thick ponytail at the base of her neck. My outsides and my insides don't match.

Or maybe what's left on the inside is reflected on the outside. I couldn't smile if you asked me to. With the exception of everything Karen's husband, Mac, does for me, I haven't had many reasons to smile in years.

I flop my long hair out over my coat. The end smacks between my shoulder blades. As I'm buttoning up, it happens. Like a moth to a flame, my gaze finds the eight-by-ten Karen keeps on the mantle.

Senior year. God-awful mottled blue background that I guess is supposed to resemble the wide sky and all the possibilities in the world. Tan sport coat, white button-down, and red-bordering-on-burgundy tie because that's the   kind of momma's boy Ellis was that he allowed Karen to choose his outfit on portrait day. Although Ellis practiced for days trying to master tying it himself. He was so proud of himself. Heck, I was proud of him.

I feel the elation of his laugh from over a decade ago, when Ellis showed me how to do it, ring hollow inside my empty chest. My windpipe collapses and the parts of my heart that had begun healing since the last time this happened once again show the telltale marks of how threadbare my life is since Ellis died.

I miss his smile. His gleaming white teeth. How he

towered over me from the moment our mothers introduced us. We had so much in common. There was never once I hadn't trusted Ellis. Whether that was showing me the secret of how to ease forked vegetables underneath the dinner table and feed them to one of his family's many animals, or slipping me the correct formula for a problem during a math test. Ellis was a constant. At seventeen, I couldn't envision my life without him. At eighteen his life was over.

So was mine.

Karen's hands rub my shoulders, breaking my trance. "He loved you. *We* love you."

"Thank you." I hug Karen, repeating the same response I've given to her and her husband whenever they've reminded me over the past few years.

What else do you say to the parents of the boy you killed?

"I love you, too" seems superficial. But *"Thank you for forgiving me for the unforgivable"* I can get behind.

Aside from Karen and Mac and my parents, I think I've lost the ability to love anyone. Some days I doubt I ever knew how to begin with.

I clear my throat and chirp, "Breakfast was wonderful. I appreciate you feeding me, but I don't want to be late!"

If Karen and I reminisce about Ellis now, we won't stop. Or she won't. I mostly let her talk out her grief and answer any questions she asks as frequently as she asks the same ones, albeit in slightly different manner. I refuse to hold things back from my best friend's mom and dad that they're entitled to know about their son. All the same, Karen and Mac own the dog training facility that I work at and she deserves an employee who doesn't shirk their responsibilities.

"It will only take a minute to get my keys?" She presses.

"It only takes a few minutes to walk that mile. The

fresh air will do me good."

"The November cold has your cheeks permanently pink, sweetheart."

"Some people call that healthy."

She releases a wry laugh. "Promise me you'll be safe. Call if you need a ride."

"I promise to be safe." We both know I won't call.

Outside, I put my earbuds in my ears, letting the music play softly so I remain aware of my surroundings. I tuck my hands inside my pockets and am down the driveway, passing the house when Karen finally goes back inside. My lips move to the lyrics and my feet fall rhythmically, landing on the wet pavement. It rained last night. I avoid the craggy puddles where the worn road dips and water fills the potholes. The weatherman says it will be sunny and thirty degrees warmer tomorrow afternoon. North Carolina's early winter weather has a serious case of ADD.

The wind whips with an icy chill as I get to the rise where the four-foot white estate fence for the training facility comes into view. A car is traveling the rutted dirt and gravel road from the building's entrance. I recognize the man in the toque who salutes me as drives past at a snail's pace. Returning his greeting with a stiff wave, I appreciate Byron's friend kept the wheels of his SUV from splashing through the nearest puddle, dousing my jeans.

There isn't much glamor in scrubbing kennel floors, but I'd hate having to explain my appearance to Byron. He's a decent guy, but even the nicest man could read between the lines and hear, "your jerk face buddy nailed me with a wall of water."

Sighing, my stomach muscles release the corded tension that builds whenever I think about the possibility of having to defend myself to him. When it comes down to it, I rarely know what to say to anyone. So, I do what I learned to do when the judge sentenced me to six years at the women's penitentiary after my best friend and I didn't make it to our high school graduation. I put my head down and hope others see it as me respecting their privacy.

But the truth is, it's really that people in general haven't stopped making what sent me to prison in the first place their business.

Byron

Week after week, Tallulah is becoming increasingly attached to Trig. I'm thrilled the Plott Hound puppy has gotten the point that he's her person the way I'm Jovie's. However, I have to keep the dogs outside a bit longer than I expected, hoping the extra playtime provides a good distraction while Trig disappears in his car.

"Good girls!" I call, clapping as Jovie mouths the ball toward Tallulah.

They're great at sharing. Tallulah takes off running with Jovie hot on her tail. I have a decent amount of concern about how my animal will react to being alone.

It won't be much longer until Trig puts a lead around Tallulah and they drive off into the sunset together. Her training is going well—and it's a heck of a lot more education than she needs as an emotional support animal—but since I started training service dogs for vets, I've become a little finicky about animal behavior. I won't let Tallulah go until she's as dependable as Jovie became after we'd dug into her drills.

Jovie's come a long way from the starving roadside

mutt I rescued and then petitioned the government to let me return with from my final tour of duty. Even before Mac offered me this job, she wasn't misbehaved. Yet once you see what these dogs are capable of, it's easy to fall into the mindset of expecting more from them. The more you love them, the more they live up to those expectations. All my dogs want in return for a job well done is praise and maybe a treat now and then.

I toss a final ball across the wide expanse of lawn. The girls go barreling after it, unaware the three of us have been the only ones playing for a good ten minutes.

My cheek sucks in on one side. My old Army buddy's stealth reminds me he has a toddler at home and he's used to leaving unnoticed. For as great as Tallulah is, any animal is unpredictable. That's another reason why she needs to be near perfect. Trig's got a family who depends on him. His wife, Kimber, agreed that a dog would go a long way to helping Trig with the PTSD he suffers from. I won't let Kimber down by expecting her to accept a dog I wouldn't consider safe enough to be around my kids. If I had any.

I whistle sharply. Jovie and Tallulah plop their behinds on the stoop at the back entrance. As soon as I open the door, they are through it. Tallulah stops to look around. She's finally figured out that Trig is missing. Her nose hits the tile floor, and she's searching for his scent. All I smell is a strong odor of disinfectant. A mop and sudsy bucket are in the hall, which means Greer is on-site.

I should correct Tallulah and the both of us should follow Jovie into my office. I'd planned on making use of my time by filing paperwork while I was here. Instead, I trail Tallulah through the hall. The pup won't find the person she's after. But I always make a point of bumping into Greer.

Greer is quiet and mindful. Impeccable at her job. Not that custodial work is hard, but it is labor intensive. I've never heard her grumble. Hell, I haven't heard a single complaint about the cleanliness of the facility since she started working here two years ago. Greer is the sort of employee that takes care of things before Mac has a chance to ask her to do it. At moments so efficient that there have been instances I've wondered if she's the ghost and not the son Mac and Karen lost ten years ago.

Any flippant remarks are best kept to myself. The three of them, Karen, Mac, and Greer, deserve to heal in peace without a big mouth butting in. It's probably why Greer's hours are odd; Early mornings. Late nights, after the vets and their service dogs have long since hunkered down to rest.

I'm about to bark at Tallulah when she crosses into the staff's break room, but become entranced by the quiet way the pup approaches Greer. The dog licks Greer's fingertips for attention. Greer turns from whatever has had her attention outside the window.

"You aren't supposed to be in here," Greer coos as she kneels down. She rubs Tallulah's ear and head and then brushes her nose against the dogs. "We need to get you out before Byron finds you."

Tallulah offers a paw.

Trust. Comfort. Whatever Tallulah sensed Greer needed, she's providing it. I'm proud of the pup. She's so close to having a loving family.

"Oh, thank you." Greer shakes it. "But I don't have any cookies to share."

Tallulah licks her snout while looking up into Greer's face. Then she inches forward to snuggle.

Good girl.

"Maybe I could take you to Byron. He's probably got plenty of treats." Greer presses a fingertip to her lips. "I won't tell him where you were. It's our secret." She shushes.

"I'm right here." I lean into the door frame. "No

bones, though. How are you, Greer?" I firmly believe she's the type who needs a friendly hello or a kind word —even if she isn't keen on relying on compliments.

"Shoot, he caught you, Tallulah. I guess you'll have to face the firing squad."

I nicker, sticking out my index finger. Tallulah rears on her hind legs, sitting straight. I aim and *"Bang!"*

Tallulah rolls to the floor and Greer's giggle tinkles in my ears.

"I shouldn't laugh when you do that, but it's so adorable." She tickles Tallulah's belly.

I join Greer where she sits criss-cross on the floor, hauling the skinny pup onto my lap with her belly up like I'm holding a baby. I rub her belly while admonishing her for being in a room that we are conscientious not to let any of the dogs in. Positive reinforcement of negative behavior isn't my go-to. But kindness matters.

"You aren't mad, are you?" Greer asks.

I'd never expect anyone on a cleaning crew to wear a ball gown. Yet it strikes me, in comparison to Karen's laid-back style after being married for thirty-odd years, that for a young woman Greer hides how pretty she is.

"Nah. I let her in, but I am going to have to make sure I keep her out so that she doesn't make a habit of it. What were you looking at?" I clear my throat. I've just given away that I've been watching Greer.

Greer's brow twitches. "The hives. Mac split two of them last summer. I'm not supposed to disturb them. Curiosity has the best of me."

"Those bees are plenty fine." Mac's voice comes from behind. "But I'll make you a deal. You can go check before you leave for the day if you let Byron drive you home," he says to Greer.

"Deal! I don't have much left to clean, Mac. I swear it won't take long." Greer jumps up from the mat she's been sitting on. She hugs Mac and scoots down the hall toward her mop and bucket.

I'm guiding Tallulah toward my office when Mac pats me on the shoulder. "It's okay I volunteered you? Greer has a proverbial bee in her bonnet about accepting a ride from Karen and scattered showers are passing through before it clears up."

"Yeah, no. It's fine. I have stuff to keep me busy until she's ready. No rush."

"Good. I hadn't found much that made that girl happy until she started helping with my bees. I'll do just about anything for Greer to smile every now and again. I appreciate your willingness to do us a favor."

Chapter Two

Byron

I'm now the distracted guy looking out the window. A sense of nervous anticipation has me poking my head up from my computer and searching the horizon to see if Greer's gone to check the hives.

I have plenty to do. Staying occupied, reading incoming applications, and sorting them based on the vets we are best suited to match with service dogs isn't the problem at all. It's more me wanting to be ready when Greer is so that she's not waiting around.

Mist shrouds the windowpane when I finally see a figure moving toward the far side of the property.

The layers of fencing Mac installed are impressive. A congenial white one greets visitors as they approach the barn-like structure. There is a shorter chain link style ones we use for outdoor lessons off the back of the building. In between is a hidden electric fence for security. His home, lacking a great barrier to keep bears out, wasn't suited for beekeeping. This place is. There's ample room for Mac's hobby and his growing collection of hives.

I grab my coat, and my dogs' attention, and we tromp

over the damp grass. Greer weaves between the tall boxes. She stoops and stands, ducking again after moving on. It reminds me of the dance the bees do themselves.

I tuck my hands in my jeans, making one-sided conversation with Jovie and Tallulah. The dogs run in oblong circles around me. They couldn't care less what I have to say. I want to make sure we're loud enough that we don't scare her.

We reach the tall oak that's shed orange and gold leaves not more than three weeks past. Underneath the empty boughs, Greer is now inspecting the feet of the wooden platforms that hold the hives. Jovie decides the water in the footholds that are supposed to keep out ants and other insects is best for drinking. Tallulah laps from a different basin.

"Those are there for a reason, not to quench your thirst!" I shoo the dogs to get them to cut it out.

They take off running in the open space. The whisper of a smile Greer has on her face fades when she glances from them to me.

It's a punch to the gut and I ease a breath out the way my granddaddy blew a steady stream of cigarette smoke from the side of his mouth.

I don't need any woman to like me. Yet I'd appreciate it if this one at least seemed slightly more relaxed that I stood on two legs instead of four.

I rock back on the heels of my boots. "Everybody still buzzing?"

"Not all of them." Greer toes the dirt.

Bee bodies litter a foot or so in front of the hive she's standing near.

I grimace. A single bee exits the hive while I'm offering my condolences. We swerve and spin to avoid the lone insect. It is a bee after all.

"This is what's supposed to happen. Those are the drones. The females push them out during the winter to conserve resources. They can't survive the cold. New ones are born in the spring." Greer stands a little taller.

"Interesting," I say because it is. "It's chilly today."

Raindrops spatter on the fallen leaves and the shoulder of my jacket. The rain picks up a notch.

"The colony stays warm. They swarm together to maintain the heat."

"Really?"

"I had a difficult time believing it myself." Greer looks longingly at the box.

"Ah, that's why you're standing in a field when it's about to pour."

"We can go," she blurts as I ask, "The rest of them are alive in there?"

"Yeah, put your ear to this one. Don't bump it. It's an active hive Mac didn't want to chance splitting at the same time as with the others. Those four on the end are smaller. They're the two he split this summer."

I lean toward the box and, sure enough, there's a faint rumbling buzz that's almost electric.

"We can go." Greer blurts again, bouncing on her toes.

"Don't want me here?"

"I'm not even supposed to be here. You don't disturb a hive in the winter. It was the small ones I was worried about. Mac let me watch from a distance when he separated them and… I just don't want anything to go wrong. A small colony is still a lot of bees to lose if they do freeze. I mean, look how many are on the ground."

"I thought those were the ones who took it for the team?"

"It's still sad." She shrugs.

At the same moment, the heavens open up. Faster than lightning crashes, the pups are already jumping up into the trunk of my crossover. I slam the tailgate and dash to the driver's door. Greer is inside, flicking water off her wet hands. I turn the engine over and direct the blower at her.

"Keep you warm. Like the bees." I kid.

She graces me with a tentative smile and polite thanks. It somehow makes me feel like we're above the clouds and she's comfortable with me giving her a ride. I don't understand why she didn't want Karen to do it. They're close.

It's not too far to Greer's place. The building is on the dingy side. My hard-wired response is to set the parking brake and lock the dogs in the car. I belatedly ask Greer if I can use her restroom and follow her inside, scanning the block for any unsavory characters. Some habits are damn near unbreakable. It was the same weary thing when Trig and I pulled up to a small village in Afghanistan.

Her key turns too easily in the lock. The apartment door is too thin. The small living room, though not unkempt, is too sparse. The elastic of the blue stretchy sofa cover nearest the bare floor has given all it's got. She's spread newsprint over half of a scratched coffee table. On top are upside-down glass bowls of various sizes that look to be drying. Green paint, glue, and glitter are to the side. A well-used brush lies beside them.

"It looks odd, but I'm building a glass Christmas tree. It's this thing I saw on Pinterest."

She feels the need to justify its significance. Whereas, I'm curious about how festive the end result will turn out. The bowls all have different etched and molded designs.

"Neat," I reply, cautious not to ask if she's adding any colors to it after it's assembled. Greer doesn't need to defend her actions to me.

"The restroom is in there. You sort of have to squeeze by the bed. Sorry."

"No need to apologize. You're doing me a favor."

The bedroom is tight. Unlike the sparsity of the living

area, a bold white Ashley-something-or-other—you know, the expensive furniture store a guy like me can never get the name straight of—fills every nook and cranny. There's about enough clearance between the full-size bed and the dresser to open the drawer. I turn and crab walk to the utilitarian bathroom; A sink, commode, and stand-up shower are all she wrote.

I don't really have to use the facilities. My elbow grazes the salmon pink shower curtain. I tip the tap to rinse my hands so that Greer is none the wiser and thinks I'm the type who never forgets to scrub. Steam rises before the water splashes into the basin. Muttering a swear word, I pull my hand away. I'm about to open the cabinet under the sink to see what the matter is when voices filter through the thin walls from the kitchen.

Greer

I'm a creature of habit, many of which were born out of necessity. My gut feeling is Byron escorted me inside because a woman on this side of Brighton may not be as safe walking to her door. He's right. I live in a shadier part of Brighton. There is a strip club mere blocks away. Everything Sweet Caroline's faces has undergone urban revitalization. Behind lies the slums. Normally, I unlock the apartment and, for as flimsy as the door is, flip the deadbolt as soon as I'm inside. Of course, Byron did the courteous ladies first gesture. And the first thing that slipped my mind?

I never relocked the door to give myself fair warning

when my landlord jiggled the handle. And unfortunately for me—right as I got my wits about me and remembered I should have also told Byron about the freaking boiling water in the bathroom—the knob turned and Waylon let himself in.

Now, we're squared off in my kitchen with Waylon arguing that he knocked, that I must not have heard him, and that he didn't know I was home. Given past experience, I'd be surprised if his nasty knuckles brushed the chipping paint.

I swear he tracks when I come and go. However, Waylon's not only big on breaking and entering—something I can't prove since he has a set of keys—he's a close talker. The kind of mansplainer who invades a woman's space.

"Can't you do this later? Now's not a great time."

Waylon has shown up to fix my sink, which wasn't broken until he was here without my consent to fix something else. I'm not a plumbing expert, though it would be slightly more believable that he was if he had a toolbox. He is only carrying a bent flat head screwdriver that's been kicked around on the sidewalk.

No lie. I kicked it myself several days in a row for shits and giggles this fall. About the time I was going to dispose of it so that no one got tetanus, the screwdriver disappeared.

I carry a pocket knife in my pants that's better suited to Waylon's current impulse. There's a butter knife in the closest drawer. A steak knife fell between the backsplash and the dish strainer. I left it there, within reach, for just such an occasion.

Waylon's insistence on being Mr. Fix-it for everything in my hole of an apartment has creeped me out for two years. I've caught him here "making repairs" on more than one occasion. I returned the small television my mom gave me when I noticed stuff going missing.

"Aaah, you got big plans I'm interrupting you from.

What you doing with all this chemicals? You making meth? Need water for that."

I bite my tongue before asking if he's an expert. He'd likely offer to help. Waylon's clothes habitually reek of cigarette smoke with a recognizable hint of pot.

Cautious not to roll my eyes, I remove the bottle with "LYE" written in bold across it from my landlord's grip and put it back in the plastic tub he snuck it out of with my wax, oils, and molds.

"I don't use drugs."

"Yeah baby, but maybe you makin' them? What's all this shit for?"

"Soap," I deadpan.

Waylon pins my thighs against the counter.

"Feeling a little dirty, girl? I can help you with that. What you say you 'an me get dirty together?"

"No, thanks." If someone else wasn't in my apartment, cold dread would fill my veins and I'd be panicking.

"Get on your knees if you want that bathroom sink fixed."

"No."

The water is the right temperature in the shower and I've taken to washing my hands that way. Sometimes the water sprays on my shirt. But it's better than grumbling and giving Waylon the reason to go into my bedroom that he's looking for. Besides, I'm pretty certain my landlord will just mess with something else, anyway.

"Bitch, you want me to tell your parole officer about the strange bottles of chemicals I found when I is fixin' shit in here."

Byron clears his throat. "Am I interrupting something?"

"Who dis?" Waylon backs off, tossing a perturbed chin in Byron's direction.

"I work with him."

"You clean dog shit, too?" Waylon bares his teeth.

Byron crosses his arms. His hard-toned biceps stretch the limits of his shirt. "I train service animals for disabled military veterans."

"You clean up dog shit." Waylon releases a bitter laugh.

"When necessary." Byron points to the door. "You were just leaving, right?"

"Yeah man, have at her. Not that you gettin' very far." Moving toward the living room, Waylon bangs Byron's shoulder. "Greer's stingy with affection. Not like dogs, who lick… your face," he adds sarcastically, sniffing the air.

Good grief, the posturing I witnessed during six years in the women's prison was more entertaining than Waylon is. Byron seems to feel the same way. He shakes his head. The scruff on his chin disappears when he brings his thumb and index finger to his lip to stop from cracking a wide grin.

"As you can tell, my landlord is a gem," I remark after Waylon leaves.

"Yeah—Um, does he normally…" Byron runs a hand into his cropped brown hair.

"Demand sexual favors in return for fixing things that I should be reporting him to Housing and Urban Development for? It wouldn't be a rainy day if he didn't." I push off the counter, thinking Byron's not interested in staying.

I wouldn't stay if someone offered me an out.

"What is all of this?" He motions to the gray tub filled with my treasured supplies.

"I'm making small batches of soap for Christmas gifts. Mac gave me the wax and honey. I got a coupon for the craft store, bought the lye and some lavender extract to experiment with."

The silicon mold, spoons, spatulas, and pot, along with a few other items, are from my favorite haunt; the thrift shop. When you are on the receiving end, the quality finds people toss in the donation bins are quite surprising.

"Where did you learn to make soap? Let me guess… Pinterest."

"The internet, so yes and no." I wiggle the cell phone my mom got me last Christmas. It's pretty handy at feeding my newfound additions; streaming television, music, and online shopping, which in my case is more like online browsing.

Although, the craft projects I find on the web are what keep me content. Minus the first, which was an epic disaster, I show Byron the progression of test batches of soap. I've intentionally kept my mistakes small since I don't want to waste the precious amount of supplies I have, and I use the not quite perfect ones that I actually managed to turn into soap in the shower. Each batch has turned out better than the last. He asks why I'm not wrapping these particular bars and I'm caught for how to explain my insecurities without bringing up my past.

Chapter Three

Byron

Her tooth wiggles into her plump lower lip. I can't tell if Greer is pleased by my compliment, or if she's retreating into herself.

She has a single sample of soap wrapped in corrugated paper with a thin ribbon and a sprig of some flower I can't name attached.

"They smell wonderful. What's not to like about them?"

"I saw soaps online and am wondering if these are good enough. There's a shop out toward the Blue Ridge that not only sells beekeeping supplies, but all handmade items from infused honey to organic lip balms. Their soap molds make my rectangular bricks seem childish. Admittedly, part of me wonders if I held the store's products in my hand if the wonders of the internet would fade."

"So go look around the shop."

"Whatever. Going all the way out there is a pipe dream and the last one I had was more like a pipe bomb that exploded in my face." Greer takes a hard swallow, seeming to regret her words as soon as they've left her mouth. "Besides, I don't drive," she scoffs.

"I could take you."

She cocks her chin, looking up at me with sudden, suspicious interest. "You *do* know who I am, right?"

"I'm aware of what happened." Mac took me aside to explain the situation when he and Karen decided to offer Greer a job.

I've been in my fair share of tough spots in my life, Trig and I lost a lot of good friends overseas, but can't imagine the shared experience my employers and this young woman have together.

It's also not my place to judge. Mac and Karen are fair and, as an employee, Greer hasn't caused any problems in the least. It's actually the opposite.

"Oh." Greer blinks and I notice how long her eyelashes are.

"Think it over. I haven't been to the mountains in ages. As for the water, Trig recommends a guy—"

Greer cuts me off. "I can't afford a guy. Waylon's supposed to repair things. Mostly he breaks more than he fixes." She rolls her eyes. "It's not a big deal. You're the only person who's been inside, other than my mom when she drops me off. I'll warn her. I'm sorry it slipped my mind to mention it to you." Her cheeks flush.

I had the feeling Waylon was as dangerous as Greer's hot water situation.

"What I was about to say was 'but how about we use that phone to search how to fix your bathroom faucet?'. I have a sneaking suspicion it's not as difficult as you may think, and I'd rather not see anyone get burned." I insist. "You gave me a lesson in bees. Let me teach you the finer points of searching YouTube and indoor plumbing."

"Ah, your dogs are still in the car. Want to bring them up?"

Certain she's saying this to get rid of me, I take Greer

up on the invite. The girls freely roam the apartment, poking their noses where they don't belong. We wind up playing with Tallulah and Jovie before they settle on the sofa alongside us and we get down to the nitty-gritty. I'm having a nice afternoon for what was supposed to be a quick drop-off.

Greer unlocks her cell. I tell her what to type in the search bar. The videos load and her jaw drops.

"That's it?" She scrambles past me into the bedroom.

I can see the soles of her shoes when she kneels and flings the cabinet under the sink open. There's an audible squeak when she turns the valve. And I swear if this were a PG movie she'd have called Waylon that "sneaky, good for nothing..." but what she does call him is deserved.

"I feel like an idiot!"

"You shouldn't. Trig shut off the hot water on me as a joke when we roomed together in the Army. And these videos are posted for anyone who is stuck with a problem or learning how to master a skill. Now that you've got water valve opening down, I'm counting on you to be the official second set of hands for plumbing issues at my house."

Greer snorts. "Doubt you live in a hole like this."

"I can assure you, Greer, I've lived in places worse than this."

"Yeah, me too... Obviously."

I won't bite. Having a who-had-it-worse contest with Greer is an insult to both of us. Instead, I sit back down on the couch, rub Tallulah's ear, and ask Greer to tell me more about the shop she wants to visit.

The subdued excitement Greer gives off is a one-eighty from the pensive and polite woman who mops and scrubs the training center until it shines. I like both sides of her quiet personality. However, the enjoyment she seems to get from showing me the products at the store is like a part of her is trying to unravel a knot that she's stuck in. Telling me about all the things she could make with beeswax, Greer makes me interested in seeing it for myself.

Her past troubles aside, she's got a good head on her shoulders. She's creative and a quick learner. And based on the sink repair and the green paint for the glass dishes she's attempting to create a pine tree out of, resourceful.

It hits me that if I change the course of the conversation ever so slightly we may both get something we need out of a trip to the western part of the state.

Motioning to her assemblage of bowls and plates I ask, "Did your family ever cut down a Christmas tree?"

"No, we got them from the Christmas tree lot in Brighton. Why?" She gives me a queer stare.

I rub the scruff on my chin as if there's something caught in my whiskers. "I don't have one and Christmas is coming up. The best place to cut your own is in the mountains. We could drive out there next weekend. Chop down a tree for me and stop into this shop for you."

"I've only cut wildflowers. Do you trust me with a hatchet?"

"Whoever said you'd be cutting it down?" I nudge Greer's knee.

Her lips twist to the side and she casts her eyes away. I see in an instant that she worries a lot about a lot. Including people's perceptions of her.

"I trust you," I say to ease the sting of rejection I hadn't meant for her to feel.

My words make her turn her head and she refocuses on my face. It's unusual that someone in her late twenties doesn't seem to know how to respond to kindness. Until I touched her knee, I couldn't have told you that it was an attempt at flirting. It's obvious that concerns her, too. I've pushed too far. Yet, I still really want to do something nice for this woman.

"I've never cut a Christmas tree myself either, so maybe two friends can figure it out together?"

Greer

When my parents moved away from Brighton, my mom kept my bedroom set. The bed I sleep in was in my childhood room. A much larger room than this is. On a much different side of town where the lawns are lush and green year-round and the neighborhoods twinkle with thousands of lights on every house at the holidays.

Some mornings—in that space between asleep and awake—I think I'm some place else. I don't always think I'm going to sit up, stretch, and slide my feet over the edge of the bed, my toes wiggling into the plush carpet. A lot of times, I'm confused as to why the mattress in my cell is plush and firm or why my body wants to cozy down under the thick comforter. When the previous day has been especially trying and I've slept fitfully, my mind places me stiffly back in a hospital bed with tense muscles, sore from broken bones... And the sinking sensation that my heart is about to swan dive off a cliff.

Even at rest, I've never been able to shake the knowledge that Ellis is gone. Although, my brain attempts to shield me sometimes. I'm both thankful and resentful of those moments because when the blinders are pulled off I feel the echo of my wailing bouncing off the hospital walls in my chest. Thinking back on my mom telling me about the accident, piecing together that I was responsible for taking my best friend's life, still has the air rushing from my lungs.

The alarm interrupted me today at the tail end of a dream. I was at the prom, but it wasn't the one I remember attending. Ellis was holding my hand. Ilona, who I bunked with at the correctional institution, had on a gorgeous blue dress that sparkled under the mirrored globe in the center of the dance floor. Her hair was pulled up in a chignon. She touched my forearm, telling me with the slightest hint of glee that my bees had escaped, which made no sense. The bees belong to Mac. But in a dream not a lot makes sense, does it?

Byron was there too. He kept trying to talk to Ellis.

I kept saying, "but he's dead."

Ellis and Byron would listen, then turn back to their conversation. I don't know why I knew Ellis shouldn't have been talking to the people I've met after his death.

However, Waylon showed up in the dream as I was failing to silence the alarm buzzer and the reason why he appeared is one-hundred percent believable.

I stewed on it before I went to bed. I tossed and turned trying to put it out of my head while falling asleep. I scrubbed my face and my teeth with a vengeance getting ready for work. I shoved everything I needed today in my backpack as if my clothes had personally offended me. My boots hit the pavement hard on the way to the five am bus and stomped the last few minutes down the road from the bus stop to the training facility.

I stand straight, angling the mop away from me with one hand and placing the other on my hip. My biceps ache from scrubbing the floor in the kennels with vigor and after holding my shoulders so tight they'd count as earmuffs.

I want to go back to bed and when I wake up I want a mulligan; on my life, on this week, I'd even bargain just for the split second when I stupidly agreed to go to the mountains with Byron. Yet, I have a keen understanding that's not the way it works.

So following through and to not disappoint Byron before his tree search begins is the least I can do.

His initial invitation excited me. I even finished my glass Christmas tree after Byron left that evening thinking about decorating his tree at his place. Not that garland and tinsel were part of the offer. I'd just concocted that little delusion.

I'd also really, *really,* want to get a thing or two at the bee shop. Nothing big. A sampler maybe to see how the owners had packaged it together. The colors, the labels, ingredients. I'd like the gifts I give to be as nice. I guess snapping a photo with my phone to refer back to will have to suffice.

Finished with my first task, I steer the wheeled bucket with the mop handle into the hall. Kicking the triangular stopper out of the day with my toe, I let the door slam. I lean back against the wood and sigh. My fingers tuck into my back pocket for the crumpled piece of paper I've been carrying around. No matter how many times I've read it, the information hasn't magically poofed in my favor.

"What ya got there?"

I jump, clutching the letter to my chest. Then I wad it up and shove it back into my pants. "You freakin' scared me!"

My heart speeds up when Byron smirks. Feeling warm and nauseous, I place a palm to my forehead.

"Greer, is it something serious?"

That all depends on who you are. For me, who lives paycheck to paycheck, it's a big deal. Waylon upped my rent. By a lot. I'm in a catch twenty-two, not able to afford anyplace else and not able to tell Waylon to go fuck himself every time he tries to come on to me.

"I got it covered. You're here early." At seven am, it's pitch black out. My hand is still rubbing my temple when it dawns on me. "Hold on, didn't you ask for the day off?"

We'd agreed to meet at the training center after my shift was over. I have an extra shirt and pants in my backpack. Plus zipper storage bags to stick all the clothes I'm wearing now in. I don't want the car reeking of Pine Sol. Although, we're chopping down a tree and pine is pine, right? Maybe Byron wouldn't notice.

"Long drive ahead of us. I figured an extra pair of hands might get us on the road sooner?"

"I get paid by the hour."

"I passed it by Karen."

My tooth wiggles into my lip and I tip my chin up, ready to argue. "She's okay with this?"

"As long as the job is done, you're golden."

Chapter Four

Byron

Two hours and two phone calls later, Greer agrees to leave early for the mountains. She had to call Karen once to confirm my side of the story—that I could help her with the tasks to get done sooner—and Mac answered a second time when Green informed him we'd finished up everything.

On speakerphone, Mac sounded impatient, pleading with Greer to just go. It wasn't the end of the world if we hadn't gotten to everything. Whatever was leftover could wait for tomorrow.

I honestly believe we did more than what Greer would have in a given day. While I popped a load of washing into the training center's machine and folded what was already dry, she kept finding nooks and crannies to dust. Extra things were sprayed and wiped down. Non-existent stains were as transparent to me before she attacked them with gusto as they were after.

She gave me the loser tasks and took most of the grunt work for herself instead of spreading the wealth around. I wouldn't have minded scrubbing a toilet bowl or mopping the floor. Latrine duty wasn't the pinnacle of my Army career, but I'm not above doing it.

Greer stares out the passenger window. She's nibbling on her index finger. I notice her fingernails are short and consider reaching across the console to remove her hand from her face.

Normally bound at the nape of her neck, Greer's blonde hair spills over the shoulders of the thick red sweater she changed into before we left. I've been hoping for a glimpse of the circumspect smile she had on at her apartment telling me about organic bee products. However, the single nudge I'd given her was proof positive Greer is uncomfortable being touched.

This isn't a date. Just two friendly people sloughing off the loneliness the season highlights. I'm definitely not trying to impress her. Nor am I enamored by the color of her cheeks. Whether she's overheated from cleaning, stomping her feet from the cold, or embarrassed, the natural rosiness isn't something I've begun to notice.

"I've been looking forward to this all week." I fiddle with the radio, breaking the ice.

She turns startled, almost as if she's forgotten I was driving the car, and hesitant in replying, "Me too." She moves her hands, fiddling them in her lap. "You didn't bring the dogs. I thought they went everywhere with you."

"They are my entourage, aren't they? I do go out on my own. The separation is good for them." I pause and breathe out heavily. "Not sure how Jovie is going to handle it when Tallulah goes to her forever home. It's starting to stress me out, actually."

"Why not get another?"

"Nah, training Tallulah was a favor for Trig. Jovie is my girl. She's getting up there. I wouldn't want to add another puppy into the mix and have it take away from our last few years together."

I owe Jovie that much for her undivided attention. I'd

been intense, focused on jumping through hoops to get her stateside and simply having my dog when I got back from my last tour. Both of my parents passed away while I was enlisted. The fact that someone was there to love me unconditionally probably saved my life. Hell, reading the article the base newspaper wrote about what it took to get Jovie home is the reason Mac and Karen introduced themselves to me. It's how I got involved in training service animals for vets.

Once you get me on the subject of the dogs and the vets we serve, I'm unable to hold back. Enlisting at eighteen, I was as lost for what to do next as I was when I'd separated from the Army a decade later. But, being raised on a farm, I love animals and I took to my current job like a fish to water. The path may be unconventional, yet I'm certain this is what I was put on this earth to do.

Greer listens intently. I recognize I'm monopolizing the conversation and try to provide indirect opportunities for her to open up about herself. She stays silent. My side cramps up underneath my ribs. I shift in my seat, trying to respect her privacy and unnerved that she might find me boring.

I am older than Greer is. Maybe that's the issue. Yet, the female friends that Trig's wife has introduced me to have been younger than Greer and they're a chatty bunch. Or perhaps since many of them work at Sweet Caroline's, those women are livelier and skilled at flirting. It does help if you're a stripper and accustomed to knowing exactly how to ensnare a man's attention.

My throat goes dry and I pick up my hours-old coffee that's in the cupholder.

"Is that from Baked Beans?" Greer rolls her lips.

"Uh, yeah. I got it on the way in this morning. It's cold. I'd offer you a sip…"

"Would you mind?" She picks up where I trail off.

"Knock yourself out."

The cup passes between us. Greer closes her eyes, pressing the recycled plastic lid to her mouth. She releases a sigh of contentment after the single sip, placing the coffee back in the spot in the console between us.

"I took my mom to Baked Beans once. They have the most amazing—"

"Chocolate croissants," we say at the same time.

Suddenly, we have something in common.

"Trig's stepdaughter is a barista there. She's got purple hair," I say, stumbling over the fact that I'm not sure how else to describe the complexities of their relationship. Then I wonder if calling out the shade made me sound like a guileless geezer who can't accept other people's life choices. I bite my tongue before doing something as insane as complimenting Greer's appearance in a lame attempt to get myself out of the hole I'm digging.

"I saw her. I thought she was very pretty."

And just like that, it's gone and Greer is pensive, finding the scenery of more interest than my company.

Greer

I slam the passenger door and codfish a few times before I can finally push the words out of my mouth.

"I'm sorry."

"You aren't the first person, with the help of the wind, to shut a car door too hard." Byron shrugs off my apology.

"I'm not good company. This thing happened last

night that I haven't been able to get off my mind. And cars make me anxious." *And men make me just as nervous.*

It's better to leave that part out, though. We're almost two hundred miles from Brighton. The last thing I need to do is offend Byron any more than I have and wind up hitchhiking across North Carolina to get home.

Stupid, run-down home that it is. It's still nice to have something to call my own. A place to go where I don't have to worry I'll be recognized, and where I can just be the crazy mixed up me that's just south of terrified of driving in a car and a map dot away from quaking in my boots each time Byron rubs the scruff on his chiseled chin.

"Okay," he says, handing me the ax.

Byron shuts the hatchback, surveying the area the Christmas tree farmer has instructed us the evergreens the size Byron wants for his living room are.

"That's it? *Okay?* I tell you I'm a nutcase and you turn your back on me while I'm holding a sharp object."

There hadn't been a point where I'd seriously gotten into any scuffles with other inmates. However, I knew how to defend myself against Waylon's advances because I learned how to in prison.

A throaty laugh escapes Byron. "Are you planning on bludgeoning me to death?"

"No." I use the duh voice I often used with Ellis when we were kids.

"Okay, so—We find a tree and you work out whatever aggression you have on it to see if it makes you feel better."

"That's it?"

"That is it. For what it's worth, I'm sorry I didn't pick up on the fact that you weren't a fan of cars."

"I can sit in one." Sort of. The ride he gave me home was quick and easy with the dogs as a distraction. This trek to the mountains was a stretch. I haven't traveled as far since I was a teenager. "Don't offer to teach me to drive."

It's non-negotiable. I will never be responsible for getting behind the wheel of a four thousand pound machine ever again.

"Duly noted." Byron nods. He rubs his palms together, then points up an incline. "Start looking over there? I'm not sure about you, but I feel like the sooner we get a tree, the faster we can find some grub. Between cleaning and the ride out here, those few swallows of coffee aren't cutting it for me."

"How long does it take to chop one down?" I shrug, unable to admit I'm hungry, too.

"Seeing as you have pent-up aggression to work off, less time than it will take to secure it to the roof."

We make our way up the hill. Byron touches the boughs of trees that are about his size. Six feet or so. He wants my opinion. The ones I chose are shorter and slimmer.

He picks up a fallen branch. "Imagine this with one red bulb dangling off. Jovie could have brought me this in my backyard."

I roll my eyes. "I get your point. No Charlie Brown trees."

We stroll a little further and I suggest one that's squat, but full. Byron agrees and I unsnap the ax's leather blade cover. He pushes up the boughs and gives me the Boy Scout version of how to create a wedge with the blade.

One strike later, I have to tighten my grip on the handle. The second blow chips off bark. The third whack and the ax gets stuck. I have to shimmy it out.

"This is harder than it seems."

"Most things in life are. You're doing fine. Once we have it started on this side, I'll move to the other and bring it down."

"Teamwork."

"It's the word of today." Byron smiles unabashedly.

It's only because we're both squatting down that I notice his lower front teeth are slightly crooked. All the others line up perfectly. His eyes are brown with the same fleck of gold and red that make up his perpetual five o'clock shadow. That hadn't passed me by before, but at the moment, it seems to matter more.

There's an odd whooshing in my ears like the drum of the laundromat washer's first slushy spin cycle rotations. With my left hand, I push at flyaway hairs, smoothing them behind my back. There's something wrong with me. I've gone from the breeze blowing through my new-to-me cable-knit sweater to wanting to yank the collar for the heat to escape before I pass out.

Steadying my breathing, I take several more swings at the trunk. Byron and I stand and he shoos me to the side. I tuck my hands under my armpits. Hearing two knocks of the ax and a crackling snap, the tree lands tip to my toes. I jump back a little, feeling girlie for doing so. And by that I mean, the old school don't-get-your-dress-dirty kind, not the new butt-kicking female superheroes that became the norm when I took a hiatus from pop culture.

Byron ignores the abundance of femininity and we drag the tree back toward the car to be wrapped and tied to the hood.

The whole time I'm hauling, rolling, and hoisting; doing exactly what I'd do if I were chopping down my own Christmas tree alone, I'm bothered by my reaction to the tree playing spin the bottle with me… And what my reaction would really be if Byron paid attention to me the way a man does a woman.

Chapter Five

Byron

It was naive of me not to recognize Greer might have a problem with cars. Not having been in any motor vehicle accidents myself, that didn't click in an instant the way the hair on the back of my neck prickles hearing a gun cock when entering the shooting range. I also still brace myself the night of the Fourth of July when fireworks go off. So had I considered what it's taken to deal with my own triggers—no pun intended— I would have cued into hers right away.

I'd wanted to make up for causing her any distress and suggested lunch at a little restaurant I'd seen coming into town. She said she was happy with fast food and ordered off the value menu, refusing to let me cover the tab for both our meals. That bugged me because this trip was my brainchild. But I guess Greer is independent, and I hadn't wanted to push her since she was still rather quiet on the car ride there and quick to get her seat belt off when we arrived.

I half expected her to bag out on going to the bee shop entirely, which was the whole reason for getting her out here. However, after she white-knuckled while I parallel parked on the street about a block down from the store, Greer suddenly had a spring in her step. One I haven't even seen when she runs off at work to take care of something for Karen, Mac, or any other employee who needs her help.

The inside of the shop is rustic. Repurposed barn timbers are used as shelving to hold honey in all its sweet and glorious golden forms, and pretty bee knicknacks are housed under domed cloches. There are soaps inside enormous glass jars with glass lids like you'd see in a penny candy store. Each one has a hand-lettered tent card beside it with the scent and list of ingredients written in calligraphy. I wander between the lotion, shaving, and beard oil displays that are all situated on waist-height vintage electrical wire spools. The wood surface is scratched and dented, adding to the naturalistic appeal.

I watch Greer out of the corner of my eye. She hesitates to touch anything at first, but the excitement slowly builds. After a while, she's picking up bars of soap and delicately examining carved and hollowed soap dishes and the cardboard packaging surrounding sample gift sets. She places a particularly large one down with a grimace and moves onto bottles of salves and lip balms.

From across the room, she shows me a tiny container with a black lid of something called royal jelly. Whatever it is piques her interest and her contained enthusiasm has me casually strolling over to check it out when she moves toward the supply bins for do-it-yourselfers. There's a premium on handmade, organic items. Although, I nearly choke at the price tag on the jar of royal jelly. It makes the large gift set look affordable. I place the jar back down, cautious not to tumble the rest of the display that's been set up in a wide triangular wall.

"This stuff is all so perfectly packaged," she says,

looking over her shoulder at the main room. "Their lip balms come in tins. I have enough wax to make some myself, but the plastic tubs they sell in this section to put them in aren't as appealing now that I've seen them the other way."

"Can you make a label for the top?"

"I suppose I could, but having the few I'd need printed would cost an arm and leg."

I'm smart enough to stop my mouth from rattling off that she can print them at home. Greer doesn't have a printer. Or a computer, for that matter.

I spy a bulk bag of empty snap-locking lid tins similar to the ones the store sells pre-filled. Geez, the cost of making things from bees seems to be about the same as buying the finished product. From the perspective of a guy who couldn't tell you what brand of bathroom soap he drops into his cart at the supermarket, this shop has a great racket going. Especially since I'm in a buying mood.

"Do you have enough wax to make more lip balm than you need?"

Greer mumbles something about Mac telling her all she has to do is ask if she runs low. "I don't want to take advantage."

"What if I get the tins and you fill some for me as gifts? And if you'll part with the soaps you were experimenting with, I'll swap the rest of the bag for those as well." Don't ask me why I'm playing Santa. According to the store's pamphlet, I'm going to have silky smooth skin and supple lips for quite a while if I don't find anyone to give it all to. Just what a guy wants, right?

She grudgingly agrees. I place the bag of tins in a round peck wooden basket with a metal handle that's nicer than any plastic grocery shopping basket I've ever used. Greer picks out a scented oil from the supply shelves and returns to choose a gift sampler from the main store. She's conscientious about separating our purchases to either side. Obviously uncomfortable with charity, when Greer approaches the register I keep it friendly, but am quick to remove what's mine and pay first.

Greer collects her change from the cashier and turns to where I'm waiting by the exit. A man focused on the display nearest the front of the store a few feet away from me bumps into her. He begins to apologize, but does a double take.

"Hey, I know you. You're, you're—" Tall and wide-shouldered, he snaps, pointing a finger at her. "Greer Rutherford. We graduated together."

Greer's face turns white as a ghost. She swallows and the action makes me aware of how fast her pulse is racing in her neck.

"Oh, my god. You're the girl who... Didn't you go to jail? Did you get out or something?"

Every set of eyes in the store is glued to where Greer stands in stunned silence, unable to move past the man. He's actually waiting for her response and, in utter disbelief at the scene he's causing, so are they.

I'm not the least bit considerate, slamming my shoulder into the guy's, allowing Greer room for escape. "If you'll excuse us."

"Dude, man!" he calls after us. As if I was the rude one.

Greer

Byron doesn't touch me. He doesn't say anything at all.

He just escorts me to his car. The only sound I hear is the chip of the alarm disengaging. There's a breeze, but I don't let the door slam. We sit in deafening silence.

I'm chilled, yet sweating, unable to focus on anything but the laces of my boots that still had the original tags on when I bought them at the thrift shop. The oil and gift sets are by my left heel. The cashier had folded the bag with a gorgeous hand-stamped beehive on it before she slid it toward me. I'd meant to save it. However, where my fist clenched created wrinkles at the top, turning something beautiful into trash.

We shouldn't have come here. Lunch and the two things I bought cost more than I had to spare. A normal person would've offered the ten I spent from my wallet for gas. I don't drive, so the thought is belated.

He puts the key in the ignition and I reach for my seatbelt, snapping it over my body and into the buckle. But then Byron leans back in his seat and places his hands on his knees.

I'm about to offer for him to leave me here. He didn't deserve the embarrassment I brought on either of us. My cheeks flame. This is why I don't go places. I even learned to avoid churches on Sundays after a similar interaction with a mother who had a toddler on her hip. Though I didn't remember her, Ellis and she were classmates. She was vehement in her unwillingness to forget what I did to him. It wasn't the first time that "Let he who is without sin cast the first stone" was less scripture and more of a script the holy can ad-lib to suit their version of the facts.

I went to jail for killing Ellis. My best friend. A boy I loved before I knew what love was. And lost before understanding we'd both miss out on the chance to love the way we were truly meant to love another human being.

According to the State, I've paid for the crime I committed by serving my sentence.

But whenever I apply for a job or see someone from my past, I'm not Greer of "Greer and Ellis: two peas in a pod" anymore. I'm a felon. Everything I'm capable of doing doesn't make a difference. It's what I *did*. I am judged every second of every day of my life by a mistake I made when I was eighteen.

By now, I should be used to the stinging reminders like today's that happen when I'm minding my own business. I'm still breathing when my best friend hasn't drawn a breath for over eight years. I'm to blame for stealing the brightest spots in our futures. I choose to own that responsibility at the sake of my happiness because Ellis hasn't laughed or cried or carried a diploma across any stage while Karen and Mac cheered him on. I did this to us and to our families.

I just wish…

"What do you wish?" Byron interrupts my thoughts.

I glance at him, startled that I'm not alone and stunned at how wet my face has become. He's watched me cry as my emotions have spiraled unchecked.

"Tell me, Greer."

Byron's expression is genuine and sympathetic, encouraging me to be honest. Despite how self-centered the emotion is, putting him in an awkward position where Byron has had to rescue me from the shop and then watch me come unhinged warrants nothing less.

"That somebody knew what it was like to kill someone you hadn't intended to."

My attention snaps to Byron's face when he replies, "I do."

He frowns. "I won't pretend it's the same, but I served and I did what my superiors trained me to do and… I know what it's like, Greer. And at the same time, I don't because for me it wasn't an accident the first time or the second… And, since I'd never want you to think less of me, I don't have the heart to tell you how high the body count is. Because… Well, it doesn't matter the circumstance or what anyone else says, taking someone's life isn't anything you get over. Not if you're a good person deep down, anyhow."

More fat tears tumble down my cheeks. My lips twist trying to form a *thank you* without my voice cracking.

He raises his arm and just as his palm is about to encase my fist which is laying on my lap, Byron stops. "If you ever want to talk about it or Ellis, I'm here to listen. No pressure. I understand being cautious about opening up. I'm the same way; The counselor at the VA when they can fit me in. Trig in a pinch when I feel myself sinking. Everyone needs a friend they can count on now and then."

I turn my hand face up and let Byron's fingers lace into mine. He squeezes and a rush of warmth flows up my arm.

The moments are few when I'm not overwhelmed by the feeling like my heart will forever be as hollowed out as a paper hive hanging outside in the winter. That the flimsy chambers will be crushed and torn down by some well-meaning person before the bees return, seeking a place to stay and renew the garden they helped blossom the previous spring. I feel that for a fleeting second at Byron's compassion.

And then it's gone. Replaced by the trilling buzz of my phone and my parole officer's voice on the other end of the line.

Byron

"Soliciting!" Greer lets out a high-pitched yell.

Behind the frosted glass, I see her jump up and begin to pace.

We drove directly back to Brighton after receiving the call from Phil, her parole officer. Do not pass Go. Do not collect two hundred dollars. Do not revel in the merciful moment when both of us were one infinitesimal step closer to closure from wounds that haunt us. Or the flicker that anyone, let alone either of us, deserved more from humanity than we oftentimes are given.

Silent and stoic, ready to accept the guilt laid upon her—for who knows what since Phil refused to say over the phone—are the best words to describe Greer along the miles we traveled back through the Piedmonts. She's been in his office for less than three minutes.

I meant what I said to her. I have a solid concept of what it's like to take a life you hadn't meant to. I didn't enlist seeking a gun and carte blanche to mow down my enemies. My not quite twenty-year-old conscience hadn't fully absorbed what I'd done until the body that

I'd shot at slumped to the barren ground. Charged with doing my duty for my country, each instance was the hollowest of victories. And then there were the kids that never got to grow up. Oftentimes, I wonder if anyone remembers them. If their families are still around to mourn the way Mac and Karen do their son. And the one thing that gives me solace is that, though their faces are patchy for timeworn memories, I remember them. I still grieve their lost innocence as I lament over what was my own.

People insist what I did in comparison to Greer's accident was different. And I can concede they have the right to their opinions. I fought in a raging war. It was survival and supporting the mission at all costs. She was a stupid kid that made a stupid mistake. I was a stupid kid doing what an adult I held in esteem told me to do, not understanding the consequences of my actions would haunt me in a similar way. The world rages on around her, and Greer—a woman now—is stuck in the same place she was at eighteen. Meanwhile, I earned a get out of jail free card in the wild west that is the Middle East.

So yes. It's completely different. But for Christ's sake, don't mention it to the piece of my soul that remains. It tends to become a little ornery when you do.

I see the fuzzy outline of her hand draw closer to the knob.

"Sit down." Her middle-aged parole officer's voice commands before she can escape the tiny room.

I rise from the molded seat I thought offices stopped decorating their waiting rooms with during the eighties. Marching over to knock, I don't bother waiting to turn the knob and enter.

"Mind if I—"

"Are you her lawyer?" Phil has an unrestrained smirk. He doesn't need to base his assumption on my brand of casual weekend attire, her parole officer knows I'm not.

"No."

"It's up to Greer." Phil sighs, putting his hands behind his head and leaning his weight back. On its last legs, the stained office chair creaks with age.

Relief apparent, she nods to the spot next to her.

"Waylon filed a complaint. He says I've been luring men to my apartment to have sex with them. The only person besides him and my mom whom I've invited inside is you." Her nose scrunches. The reality is her landlord doesn't need an engraved invitation or stand on formality. Greer affirmed to me that Waylon comes and goes as he pleases.

"Are you Greer's boyfriend?"

"Just a friend from work," I supply, rubbing my chin. Greer hasn't asked me to defend her, but there's no reason not to. "The first time I was at Greer's place was to drop her off earlier this week. I asked to go inside to use her restroom. On the way back to the kitchen, I overheard Waylon propositioning Greer in exchange for getting her bathroom sink fixed. He wasn't happy to find me lurking in the doorway behind him, and while I can't prove anything, it stands to reason that Waylon was the one who caused the issue in the first place."

"What makes you so sure?"

"Aside from a roll of toilet paper, there was nothing else in the sink cabinet. Whoever did it turned the cold water valve off, risking someone getting burned." Pause letting *like me* hang in the air and hoping the guy is smart enough to surmise *like her*, too. "Those knobs don't just turn on their own."

"Where's this sink located?" Phil asks, jotting down some notes.

"In the bathroom off of the bedroom," she states.

The man looks up, not at all surprised at Greer's answer, and drops his pen. "Has your landlord asked you to engage in sexual congress at any other time?"

"I don't know. Maybe... yeah," she whispers, picking

a nonexistent pill from her red sweater. Her eyes roll back and close and her face blanks, concentrating on trying to find a way to fix her problem.

"My advice is to find someplace else to live."

"I can't afford to stay, anyway. Waylon upped the rent on me." Greer shifts, taking a folded paper out of her pocket.

"When?" Phil reaches across the desk with a gimme motion.

"Yesterday."

He blows out a breath and shakes his head. "Listen, Greer, I'm investigating this on my day off because I never hear a peep about you unless it's when I confirm your employment status. Those people at the dog center like you. They never have anything bad to say. If you were my daughter, I'd tell you not to bother going back to the apartment tonight—especially not alone. This is the type of person who, once he gets his nose bent out of joint, is likely looking to cause an issue. So, if you do keep living there, and Waylon doesn't find another thing to drive you out sooner, expect to be right back here, accused of doing something else. And next time it won't be some jerk-off's complaint. Waylon will bring me whatever proof he can to back it up."

Greer

Byron lives on the side of town that Sweet Caroline's faces. There are speed bumps and signs cautioning children at play. Happy people here lead a contented existence, doing the things they were destined to do;

buying milk on the way home from their nine-to-fives, teaching the babies they are raising to pedal a bicycle, paying off student loans, and saving for the future.

The neighborhood is filled with identical single-story houses in yellows and blues. Byron's is tan, but the sun casts a pink hue and my mind runs through the refrain from a John Mellencamp song—the only line of lyrics I know—before it launches into *American Kids* by Kenny Chesney.

I'm standing in his backyard, throwing a ball to Jovie and Tallulah. They chase the ball toward the fence line that has towering pines behind it, jumping and playing. Every burst of energy makes me feel awful that they were cooped up even longer today because of me. Tallulah spits the ball at my feet. It rolls over the toe of my boot leaving a smear of drool, yet I don't think twice about picking it up and throwing it for them again.

I'd like to ignore Byron's penchant for collecting strays. However, not sure what to do with me, Byron brought me home. He let the dogs out. We untied the tree from the roof and braced it against an empty corner in the living room. He showed me how his washer and dryer worked so that I can wash what I wore cleaning this morning and have fresh clothes for work tomorrow. And then, because I'd been stewing in the car, and my emotions got the best of me, I had what's probably the most embarrassing breakdown in recent history.

"Greer, you can talk to me about it."

"About what? That my landlord accused me of prostitution? We both know that's ludicrous! But what am I supposed to say to defend myself and what does it matter, anyway? Even if I still had a shitty place to live, who's going to believe that I've never been with a man?" I snarl, taking my frustrations out on the closest target.

I catch sight of Byron's face before he has a chance to stop the frown that forms. He flushes and not to be outdone, my cheeks turn brighter than the sweater I'm wearing.

"I didn't just say that." My palm slaps my forehead. "It's not. I've..." I swallow. "I had a girlfriend once."

"So you're—"

Honestly, I don't know what I am. Ellis consumed my thoughts my entire childhood. A few years after he died, Ilona and I became cellmates. Prison is not a bastion of tenderness. Having someone to touch. To hold. It kept me going. Until she was gone—moved to another cell block—and I was back to being having no one to trust my heart or my secrets to, and with someone new resting opposite me.

I'm not stupid. I knew what Ilona and I had wasn't forever. But losing something precious to me a second time was enough to not seek it out a third. My luck in love is like a rickety wooden pail with a hole in it. It ran dry before the bucket left the edge of the well.

"Celibate." I finish Byron's sentence.

I'm not in or out of the closet. I'm not ashamed of loving Ilona the way I carry the shame of Ellis's death. I just am. I found the beauty in Ilona's soft curves and can see it underneath the brow and red scruff in the hard line of Byron's jaw. Accepting both sides makes me who I am. And so does choosing to live my life alone since my release.

There is a deep gap in my experiences. A cavern that's virtually uncrossable because I took responsibility for my actions; a crime that will haunt me for the rest of my days. All the things I believed were on my horizon at eighteen, I didn't get to accomplish. I didn't go to college, get to have a fulfilling career, or marry my high school sweetheart.

And now I'm standing out here past dark with no place to go except a run-down apartment that the landlord wants me to pay for with my body. There's not much further to fall, so why is letting Waylon steal a piece of my soul that I haven't robbed myself of seem like the most demeaning experience I've had? After all, people belittle me for an impulsive decision I made nearly a decade ago. I should be used to the disparaging remarks and insinuations that I haven't grown past the person I was. That I'll be forever stunted, rooted in place like these pines that watch the families, but are gated away by the neighborhood fences that keep everyone else safe.

The back door opens and closes. I hear the creak of a loose porch board and the shuffle of Byron's steps behind me. The dogs retrieve the ball again, bringing it to him instead, proving my point. I am an observer rather than a participant.

My mind tweaks the last line of the earworm. *I'm a little messed up, but it's all alright, right?* It matters to no one. Therefore no one has to know.

Byron kneels to greet his dogs. The girls eat up the attention the way they'd gobbled their dinner.

"I got the Christmas decorations out of the attic and the tree is in the stand."

I appreciate how natural he's acting. It's as if I'm a normal friend, not the girl who can only get a pitiful job from the parents of her first love. Not the anxious passenger in the car. Not the broke woman with no place to go.

So it makes no sense when I sink to my butt next to Byron and blurt, "I kissed him—Ellis. The night he… died. I'd been holding out for him to see me as more than just his best friend. It was my first real kiss."

Byron

There's a point between prom night and graduation that I remember living on endorphins. My emotional diet was the simultaneous feeling of being high as a kite at the idea of newfound freedom and abject panic. The anxiety, being the precipice of something new and undiscovered, was enough to make a guy want to throw up. Those short weeks compressed more of the highest of highs and the lowest of lows than I'd experienced to date all wrapped up in a tidy bow I'm now able to give a name to: Anxiety.

I drank and smoked and lied to my parents about situations I thought they'd never understand. Like stumbling late into a final with a pounding headache and hangover that lasted past when the teacher said, "pencils down."

My dad and I spent a lot of time together the summer before I left for boot camp. He ran a small farm northwest of Fayetteville that I returned to when I was stateside and subsequently sold after my parents passed away as I was in no position to plow a field or harvest a crop. Though I have fond memories of growing up doing just that. Dad had done a short stint in the Army and our mirrored experiences were a natural opening to share stories of his youth that my parents protected my impressionable mind from as I was growing up.

So it doesn't surprise me that the bulk of Greer's teenage experiences were relatively the same as anyone else's.

It also seems to me that, no different than driving in the sand on alert for an ambush, Greer spends every day walking a tight wire. At least I had Trig riding next to me. Other than the occasional nightmares—mine being less frequent and severe than Trig's. Hence why I'm busting my ass, training Tallulah as the best emotional support animal possible—I've rarely worried the rope will snap.

After everything that went down today with the loud-mouthed schmuck at the store and Waylon lying that Greer was hustling men for sex, the tension must become unbearable.

I refuse to even think about the fact that Greer admitted that she was a virgin. The other part, about having a girlfriend doesn't shock me. I suppose it does make me curious about her experience; something that's none of my damned business.

The interest in who Greer is, the desire to spend time with her, and my reasons for not letting her go back to her apartment makes me aware I'm balancing too.

I like her. But is this one-sided attraction? Me wanting what I can't have? Ignoring our age, Greer and I are still co-workers. And she likes women. But she kissed Karen and Mac's son.

"My first kiss was a particularly bad round of seven minutes in heaven. We both had braces." I motion my open palm over my face. "Terrified they'd get tangled, and we'd wind up lip locked," I admit, though in all my years I've never actually met anyone who'd been a victim of this urban legend. "I hope kissing Ellis was better."

The corner of Greer's lip tips up ever so slightly and falls, recalling the memory. "We were best friends. He'd dated a few girls who I hated. I'm not sure if that's why he didn't get serious with them. Come senior year, both of us planned to go stag to the prom. School sold the tickets in pairs. For couples. So, we split the cost and wound up each other's date.

"My mom took me shopping for dresses. I stood in front of the three-way mirror at the boutique, staring at myself in a ballgown, wondering if Ellis would kiss me. That's when I realized I fell in love with Ellis all at once and over time. It didn't even bother me that Ellis kissed someone before me. Everything about it was perfect. Just like he was."

There's a peace that settles over us. Greer is quiet, reflecting on her past. I won't interrupt, holding out hope that she trusted me enough to reveal more. I'm rewarded for that patience when she continues.

"Afterwards, Ellis held my hand the rest of the night as if I'd always been his. And because I had. I would have done anything he asked just to be close to him. We were joined at the hip since the day we met. I had the most romantic notions that a single moment meant forever for us." Greer scoffs. "I'm pretty sure that I pictured my mom crying at our wedding. But the next time I saw my mom, I was waking up in a hospital bed and her tears tore me apart."

We're shoulder to shoulder, facing out into the yard. The night has grown bitterly cold. Yet Greer doesn't shiver.

My elbows rest on my knees with my hands clasped together. I turn to look at her, seeing both her youth and the faint lines stress has left marring the skin surrounding her eyes. She's so tired of living with constant unease. Being unable to sleep without waking to despair. Holding onto the fear of retribution instead of hope for a better future.

I wonder who else knows the rest of the story. If she tells it to me, will it lighten the load she's carrying?

Though defensive over what she endured today, I soften my jaw and recall her graceful movements through the bee shop. God, this afternoon seems further away than happening today.

"How did the accident happen?"

Greer meets my gaze. "We went to an after party. I drank because Ellis was drinking. I drove because he'd had more than me, and I didn't want anything to happen to his car. He'd bought it with his own money. Karen or Mac would take it away if they found out we'd had alcohol. I was too caught up in the night to even consider I'd take even more from them. The police said the skid marks proved I swerved on a straightaway, but no one figured out why. In the hospital, I couldn't remember and it's not like the reason would change the outcome." She shakes her head. "I wrapped the passenger side around a tree. Ellis died on impact."

$\mathcal{G}$reer

I wish it was me that died. But if it had to be Ellis, I wish my penance included both of us. I've thought about how that would've torn two families apart losing both their children. But hadn't I done that, anyway?

After the accident, lawyers advised Karen and my mom to only speak through them. Attorneys cost money. My dad's thriving HVAC business failed. People would rather burn through a hellish summer than give their paychecks over to the father of a murderer. My parents moved out of Brighton, to a place where no one recognized they had a daughter convicted of DUI and vehicular manslaughter. They had to rebuild from the ground up.

Me six feet under would have been best for everyone. I don't say that lightly, or with an unwillingness to bear responsibility for my actions.

But that's not what happened.

A single moment linked Ellis and me forever. It just wasn't the way I hoped.

I don't flinch when Byron lays a hand on my back. Perhaps today was just too much for me and my senses are on overload. Maybe I want the same unconditional warmth a hug from my parents brings. My fingertips are ice and I'm hunched, huddling in a ball where I sit on the hard porch boards.

Byron has left the back door open. The dogs have gone inside to drink from their bowls. The buzz of the dryer reminds me that my clothes are ready to get soiled again. It also interrupts me from apologizing for dragging Byron into my pathetic existence.

"Thank you for trusting me," he says.

"Thank you for sticking up for me with my parole officer."

Although I'm sure the finality changes little, I only have a few months left until that chapter is put to rest, and Phil isn't obliged to look in on me. The State didn't compel Byron to tell the truth about Waylon. He could have dropped me at Phil's office and left. I owed Byron the consideration of understanding who he got himself involved with.

I stand and his hot hand catches my chilled one, dropping it when I look to where we are joined.

His voice is measured when he speaks. "I want you to stay here."

Prisoners are moved without warning. I'd been taken

for exercise when Ilona was told to remove her things from our cell. *I want you to stay with me,* my heart called out at the sight of the empty institutional mattress. Afterward, I dreamed of Ellis and told him, *If you have to go, take me with you.* Each night Ellis broke my shattered heart into smaller pieces, grinning and replying, *you have to stay here.*

"I need to fold my clothes." I point beyond the glass slider. Janitor or beauty queen, I won't show up to work rumpled.

"If Waylon's kicking you out of the apartment, do you have any place to go?"

"No." My mouth moves more than I whisper.

"I want you to live here, Greer. I have an extra room. I won't charge you more than you're already paying." Byron's brow furrows.

What will his neighbors say if they find out?

"I can't do that." All I can think of is dragging my dad's business through the mud.

The parolee assistance program in North Carolina helped me get a place to live near the job Karen insisted I accept to comply with the terms of my release. I refused to darken my parent's doorstep and ask them to give me anything more than they already had. A specter, I drift through windows when I'm positive the community is safely ensconced in their personal holiday celebrations to pay attention.

Byron gets up. I have to tip my chin ever so slightly to see him. He pushes his broad shoulders back. The outdoor lighting casts his face in the most fascinating harsh shadows. My body quakes, and I tell myself I'm reacting to the upcoming winter's true temperature.

"I won't let you go back alone, even if it's to get your things." His remark is steadfast. "Your options are limited to living on the street, which violates your parole, or to live with me. Even if it's just however long it takes to get back on your feet, you have to stay *here.*"

I focus on Byron's living room through the window. He's removed the mesh netting when he placed the tree we chopped down in the stand. The green boughs have unfurled. A cardboard box with "ornaments" scrawled in black marker sits to the side.

"Here" has never sounded more like "home". And the prospect of home has never been scarier. I'll have to leave Byron's house when he moves on; Relocates. Finds a girlfriend or someone to share the most intimate part of his life with. Decides living with a ghost is too much.

I'm as removed from the scene inside the house as I am when I glide into my parents' home. But I agree to stay with Byron because I'm terrified... Of the next landlord's constant intrusions being worse than Waylon's. Of having my parole revoked. Of offending the one ally I have in the man standing in front of me. And because deep down all of my memories center around that kind of hurt, and it's easier to survive expecting it than lying to myself that Byron is offering me a place to stay forever.

Chapter Eight

Byron

I'd meant for Greer to sleep on the sofa with the tree lights twinkling. But once she agrees moving in with me is for the best, relief overtakes us and exhaustion settles in.

We decide the ornament box can remain unopened until the following day. I bring her a blanket and the spare pillow from my bed and make myself scarce. As I'm about to turn in, I have to go searching for Tallulah.

Trig's pup snuggles at the base of the sofa, nearest where Greer's head lies. From the carpet, Tallulah peers at me. Greer's hand rests on the dog's back, giving the impression she was mid-stroke patting Tallulah when she fell asleep.

Tallulah arches a single brow and then the other. Instead of asking her to mind, I wink. For as much time as I spend with my furry friends, I've never quite gotten the hang of questioning the world with the unique facial expression that only a dog can manage. Then I back off, stepping lightly down the hall. Tallulah is doing what I trained her to do. What does it teach Tallulah if I call the dog away from Greer when Greer obviously needs support?

I crack the bedroom door so that the pup can still come to lie down in her bed later on.

The sun streams in the next morning. I head to the kitchen to start the coffee. It's a bag I'd picked up at Baked Beans and keep in the freezer for special occasions. Tallulah is where I left her, but Greer is missing.

I panic until I spot her red sweater folded on top of the neat pile of linens. I slept until my alarm went off. Greer goes into work before daybreak.

I indulge in the coffee anyhow while feeding the dogs, shower, and dress. Then I leave Jovie and Tallulah behind for the second time in two days and drive to the training center.

"Good morning, Byron." Karen waves, stopping short. "Where are the girls?"

An excuse rolls off my tongue. "Not feeling well. I may take an early lunch to go check on them."

"Aw, I'm sad to hear that. Whatever you need."

"Thanks… Oh hey, Karen, have you seen Greer around?" I try to sound nonchalant.

"She's finishing up in the kennel. Nice job yesterday, by the way. I think you did more than your fair share. If this dog trainer gig goes south and you can moonlight as a custodian." She ribs.

"Appreciate it, and I'll keep that in mind." I laugh. "Greer did the hardest parts."

Karen hangs her head. "I'm sure she did."

I trod off, finding Greer right where Karen said I would. The kennels were spic and span before we cleaned in here. I can't fathom what else there is to do when the training center doesn't house any animals in between the holidays. Pups deserve a Merry Christmas too.

"You left." I kick the doorstop out of the way to give us some privacy. I lied to Karen because Greer gets to tell her what she wants.

"I wasn't sure if you needed the first and second month upfront. It's not like Waylon's coughing my security deposit back up."

I codfish.

"Kidding, Byron," Greer deadpans.

"I could have driven you in."

"One stop fewer on the bus." She shrugs. "I didn't want to wake you."

"I can drive you home when your shift is over."

"Did you know there are also nicer bus stops on your side of town?"

"Greer."

"Don't worry. I won't go to my apartment alone."

"The back of my car is empty. I'll bring you to get whatever we can carry. Trig owes me a favor. We'll get the rest and your furniture—"

Greer closes her eyes. "Why are you being so nice to me?" she asks, dropping her grip on the spray bottle and dingy newsprint she's holding.

"What have you done that gives me a reason to be mean?"

"I killed Mac and Karen's son."

"That's not a reason. And it isn't something you did to me." Those are issues she has with our employer. From my vantage point, it's clear they're healing, so why make their trauma my business?

"I only have six hundred each month to put towards rent." She deflects.

"Dollars?"

"No, dog bones. Yes, dollars."

"Waylon charged you that much..." *for that hole*, I catch myself before I say it aloud. He upped the rent, too. By how much I can't imagine. "It's just a room. I want two-fifty."

"Four. Unless I'm paying for each time my butt cheek touches the couch cushion."

I burst out laughing. She's got me on that. "Three. My mortgage isn't that high and you'll probably get dog hair on your clothes while you're watching TV."

"When don't I have dog hair on my clothes?" She motions to her attire, almost smiling. "I may even feed Jovie and Tallulah table scraps from the fridge when you aren't looking. Three fifty and I'll throw in floors and windows. Bathrooms too. Wait! You do hit the bowl, right?" Smartass cocks a defiant chin.

I snort. "Three fifty, and that includes utilities. Wait! You know what a light switch is for, don't you?" I give Greer a chance to snicker. "We share the chores, but you won't hear me complain if you run the vacuum more often." I hold my hand out.

"Is this a trick? You teach me to shake like your dogs and then add in something like you're buying all the food." She shies away.

"Greer," I repeat the growl. She's exasperating.

But she stands up for herself. She isn't asking for a handout. And I like that the banter keeps me on my toes.

"Fine."

"Thank God," I mutter when she clasps my hand.

"Tallulah sleeps with me," Greer adds before letting go.

Did she just bait and switch, changing the rules on me?

"On the floor." I keep her fingers in my grip.

"You expect me to sleep on the floor?" She teases, pressing her lips together and her cheeks flush.

Damn, she's pretty. But it's best to let sleeping dogs lie.

"I expect you to come get me when you're done cleaning so we can get your stuff. Tallulah has a bed. I'll bring it to your room once Trig and I haul over your furniture."

Greer

I took the bus home from work earlier this week. Showered and changed. And sat criss-cross on my bed looking out at the living room. I can see the TV from where I sleep and could swipe the remote to turn it on and lie back on my pillows.

But I never do.

The couch and rickety other furniture were part of the package at my old apartment. Byron and Trig left those things there. I didn't even want the sofa cover. They stored the pots and pans I cooked with in the garage rafters. Byron has his own.

Around noon, I reorganize my few possessions, fold my clothes into the drawers, and wipe down the bathroom that I use. After that, I run the vacuum in anticipation of Byron taunting me with "missed a spot" wherever the lines in the carpet disappear. I dust, and I hid for forty-eight hours that I had washed the windows. Byron grumbled at me until his stomach growled.

"What's that smell?"

"It is either Pet Fresh, Windex, or dinner," I said in a pick-your-poison manner.

"You cook?" Bryon approached the stockpot on the stove, lifting the lid and inhaling.

He'd been out the first few evenings I was here and I'd eaten the leftovers pulled from my fridge.

"Not as well as I clean. But I ran out of craft glue finishing the glass tree and got bored. I'll replace what I took from your pantry when I get out of work tomorrow." When I'd planned to stop for more glue.

I've always preferred the selection at the craft store on this side of Brighton, and the grocery stores are well stocked. Although they cost a bit more, I don't have to hoard my pennies as tightly now that Waylon isn't fucking me over.

Still holding the lid askew, he blinked. "You don't have to do that. Can we eat now?"

I agreed and somehow got talked into making dinner with Byron the rest of the week. Having someone around to chat with has been a pleasant change of pace. Sometimes he leaves the dishes to me, other evenings I do the same and play with the dogs. Last night, he turned on a movie and emptied a bag of microwave popcorn into a bowl to share. Tallulah and Jovie snuggled up on the couch between us. I might have intentionally dropped a few kernels.

"I see what you're doing, sneak."

"The popcorn bowl is on top of Jovie." So we can both reach in. "She's earning her keep."

"And Tallulah?" Byron arches a brow, grinning at the puppy with her head resting on my lap.

"Brownie points for being adorable."

I don't have much longer to spoil Tallulah. She's going to her *furever* home in January.

I got a little maudlin until Byron tossed a handful at me, breaking the spell when the girls jumped to gobble the errant popcorn.

This afternoon, I pulled my soap making supplies from the cabinet Byron cleared out for me to use in the kitchen. Christmas is swiftly approaching. My mom is picking me up to go spend the holiday with my parents. I need my gifts ready and I owe him the soaps I've already made, along with some tins of lip balm to give away.

The craft store had discounted spring silicone molds

when I was there for glue. So I bought thumbnail-sized bee and flower trays meant for candy making—not realizing I could probably make honey candies with them before scraping the remaining soap from the pot that I hadn't wanted to waste. Those teeny tiny soap buds and bees are setting along with the large bars I need to wrap.

Next up, I open the bag of lip balm tins and set up my double boiler, which is really just two pots. One I fill with water. The second fits inside the other and the heat melts the beeswax. I stir in peppermint essential oil and begin craving candy canes. Maybe flavoring the lip balm wasn't the best choice? What if people lick it off and get chapped lips? Too late. I guess we'll find out.

The tins are setting in the fridge and I've popped the tiny soaps from their molds. The flowers and bees are perfect. I wrap them in cellophane bags and tie them up with the same twine as I use on the soap bars. Byron has an overgrown holly bush in the backyard that I snap twigs from to festively decorate the larger bars.

I'm in the zone when Byron gets in from the training center.

"Look at this assembly line, Henry Ford!"

"Ack!" Still having to clean my mess, I take note of the clock. "I'm almost done!"

"Show me what you've made," he requests, sounding genuinely interested.

Soap making and basically anything bees get me buzzing, so it doesn't take much encouragement for me to sell my wares.

I pick up a pot of lip balm, gushing that I used some cheap red lipstick shavings to color it pink.

"It's not organic anymore, but I was experimenting. And I can always try to source the color online through the bee shop we went to."

Byron sticks his thick index finger into the tin, swiping more than any normal human would. He covers his lips with it.

"That's a nice shade on you." My attempt at not laughing is futile. He left a clump on his lower lip. Immediate regret seizes me, lifting my hand to spread the balm.

The flecks in Byron's eyes ignite. He grasps my fingertips, bringing my palm to his face, and he lowers his mouth over mine. His lips are slick and soft. I breathe in mint. I'm about to open mine and lick toward the candied scent that's had me craving sweets, and… Byron pulls away.

"I'm sorry, Greer, that shouldn't have happened." Byron scrubs the back of his neck. The faux slate ridges on the gray and blue linoleum have become interesting to him.

I turn toward the stove. Despite my heart stalling out and the words begging him not to apologize getting stuck in my throat, the prickle of tears overcomes every other sensation.

"You live here and… Waylon. Plus, working together. I mean—"

My voice is like a rusty door swinging its hinges. "I understand." I've managed to put one more person in an untenable situation.

"I, uh. I'm going to go shower before we make dinner."

"Don't worry about me. I'm not all that hungry," I lie.

Chapter Nine

Greer

The layout of Byron's house has the entrances to our bedrooms set apart. However, they share a common wall, as does his ensuite bath and the one I use in the hallway. Safely ensconced in my room, the rushing water flowing in the pipes is audible.

His quick shower lasts longer than any other has. He must be glad my mom is picking me up tomorrow and he doesn't have to face me when he's finished. I sure am. How do you act normal after slamming on the brakes?

There's no crab walking between my furniture, or standing to the side to rifle through my things to find my pajama shirt. The neck hole is slipping over my head when a slap against the tile in his bathroom seems to reverberate, otherwise emphasizing the silence of the entire house.

I jump, tensing the way I did while becoming used to the clanging sounds on the inside. Byron swears. Not a minute later the water cuts off and the shower door slams. I shudder a final time hearing the drawers angrily slide open and whizz shut. Despite understanding the glass tree made from bowls and saucers on my dresser is on a solid footing, the noise has me fearful it will get knocked off and break.

He can't see me, but I haven't felt this exposed and vulnerable since taking my first steps into my cell finding out Ilona was gone. If anyone asks, I now know the sting of rejection when your breakup is the forced outcome of prison guards following protocol equals that of someone apologizing for kissing you.

There are no degrees to wanting to crawl into a hole and stay there till someone a thousand years from now stumbles across your dried and picked apart bones. The desire for solitude or seclusion are involuntary. They're heartache's constant companion.

Byron reacted as if kissing me was the biggest mistake he'd ever made. Meanwhile, my body lit up, and I'd been ready to kiss him back.

One more not-so-lovely memory to add to the scrap heap.

One more rejection I wasn't aware would slice as deep as it does.

One more time I'm forced to endure my worst mistake while becoming someone else's.

I get into bed, pulling the covers to my chin and wrapping my arms around me. The room isn't cold, but my nipples are taut. I'm still flushed from embarrassment. And, dear lord, being cast aside must turn me on because I'm horny.

How pathetic is that?

Byron—who never showers before dinner—had to scrub himself clean of me and I'm raring to go.

Byron never showers before dinner.

Byron showers before we hang out at night or once I've gone to bed.

But he showers in the morning too. I've gathered the towels to wash and his hasn't dried.

Why is Byron showering if he's already clean?

My fingers kneed into my breast, the center of my palm putting pressure against my areola as if my hands are enlightened by my thoughts. Like the beeswax melting in the double boiler, heat spreads in my lower belly.

Did he… Was he… Just now…

The slap was out of frustration, wasn't it?

What was he frustrated about, Greer?

My right hand moves down my body. At the apex of my thighs, my fingertips become damp. I take a tremulant breath in. The quiver in my knees as the pads brush against my clit makes me move my head back and forth on the pillow. I burrow down, spreading my legs, stroking until my fingers are slick and the only way to quell the desire is to slide one inside.

I pick through the fantasies I've had. Ellis. Ilona. The pretend lover that grew to know my wants and desires better than I could. The people I've found myself attracted to for the briefest moment before I've recognized it wouldn't work out. They skitter to the back of my mind and in the forefront stays Byron.

I shouldn't think of him while touching myself, but trying not to is futile. A soft moan escapes me. I clamp my mouth shut. What if Byron overhears?

You heard what he was doing. I scold. *He can't judge you when he gripped his cock in his hand.*

I don't know that. Yet, my imagination paints a picture of water streaming over Byron's chest. He's bracing an arm against the tile. It morphs to him leaning over me on the bed. I'm naked. My legs are askew and the tip of him is sliding against the places my hands are traveling to.

The flutter starts as soon as I think of Byron pushing inside of me. Plunging a second finger into my channel, my lips part, and I ride out the wave. My hand clutched between my legs, I roll to the side. Little sparks shoot where I continue to rub.

If I'd kissed Byron back faster, would this have happened with him? I press my eyelids shut and let sleep overtake me.

There's no sense in revisiting the past. It changes nothing, other than understanding that since the beginning, an underlying attraction to him has made me wary and defensive. And now I have to live with those things on my conscience too.

Byron

What kind of short circuit in my wiring turned me into such a fucking numb nut that I'd kiss Greer?

She's told me she likes women. And she's a virgin. And she's celibate, so she's obviously not looking to change the fact that she's a virgin.

I respect her desire to live life on her terms without being judged by her past. She's content with quiet. Happier with making others feel special. Unwanting of any limelight, or attention at all, for that matter.

When I'm with Greer, her choices are reasonable. Away from her? My dick is in my hand. And one shower is not enough. I've freaking come in my boxers by the next morning, after chastising myself for stroking one out the night before.

Fuck you very much, subconscious, for replacing nightmares with wet dreams.

Explaining to Karen and Mac that moving into my spare room was her last option was hard enough on Greer. Not that Karen didn't offer theirs, but Greer's too proud to take any more from Ellis's parents. It's why she's punctual. Never complains. Always working like a dog. Continually thinking of others.

Greer even managed to box up the soaps and lip balms she owed me before slipping off to visit her parents. And the vacuum lines in the rug were perfectly parallel! Between the honeyed homemade soap scents and all of her tidying up, I might even forget two dogs live with us.

I've got to stop using the F-word, but it's just so un-fucking-fair that I'm obsessed with a woman who I haven't got a chance in hell with.

"You're jumping to conclusions." Trig polishes off the last swig from his beer bottle. He points to Kimber. "Tell Byron he's off his rocker, My Love."

December twenty-fourth and we've got barstools attached to our asses at Sweet Caroline's where his wife is the manager. There's a tired piece of chewing gum on the rim of my empty. It lost its elasticity on the drive here, making my jaw ache. But without it, I may have ground my molars down to nubs.

Kimber balls up a rag she's used to wipe down the bar. "I can handle giving advice to customers, but the worst is shining a light up a friend's butt."

"What my wife means is—"

"Don't you put words in my mouth."

"What about my…"

"Trig Avery!" She tosses the towel at him. "Maybe, if you're lucky. However, innuendo isn't helping Byron." Kimber leans her elbows on the bar. "You both seem indifferent to your age gap. Other than your concerns about pressuring Greer the way the ex-landlord did, nothing strikes me as an argument for Greer not being interested in you. She liked a guy once. So what that she's attracted to women? Plenty of the dancers and the clientele here are too. Who hasn't kissed a girl nowadays, even if it was just for fun?"

"Listen to My Love. She's smart. And I am the

steadfast wingman from the cheesy romance on the silver screen that will clap you on the back," Trig pauses, gripping my shoulder, "and say, 'There, there, my friend. Everything will work out'."

"You are cut off, Trig." Kimber takes a tray of drinks to serve to guests at a table nearest the stage.

"We just got here. This is my first one!"

"And your last," she sing-songs.

He reaches over the counter, filling a glass with soda water from the plastic gun. "Her hormones are killing me."

"You guys still trying?"

"For now, yeah." Trig sighs, rubbing his Temple. "Kimber wants another baby bad. I don't have the heart to disappoint her. Which means jerking off into a cup and letting her bring it to the doctor's office."

"Not a visual I needed."

"Same here. You've basically admitted to rubbing one out over a woman who has friend-zoned you."

"That's harsh, wingman." I chuckle. There's something a little less pathetic about knowing you aren't the only one with problems. "What about riding off into the sunset and happily ever afters?"

"Man, this is real life. If it weren't, I'd have knocked my wife up and you wouldn't be spending Christmas Day with my dog."

"Your dog is going to be awesome."

"She already is. She's *my* dog... Really, Byron, what you've accomplished with Tallulah is great. I would've been glad to take her off your hands months ago. Kimber and I can't wait for her to be a part of our family." He nudges me. "Forget about feeling guilty about the kiss. Chalk it up to a mistake. We all make 'em. Greer isn't the first lady you've laid one on who in the end wasn't interested. There was that staff sergeant who changed her mind about her divorce."

"You had to bring that one up?" I guffaw.

That particular woman and her spouse had separated. We dated stateside and when the manilla envelope arrived at her APO address overseas, suddenly saving her marriage was a priority. She was in contact with her husband and attempting to reconcile while emailing me. I'd seen relationships go either way while I was deployed. Some soldiers can't handle the distance and cut their loved ones off. Others hold on tighter for a connection to what's safe.

"Did because you dodged a bullet there, man. Didn't she eventually leave him, anyway?"

"He left her," I grunt with the smug satisfaction only the jilted can muster. "I'm not looking to dodge anything with Greer, though. Except putting her in a compromising position."

"You can't say for sure that's what you did. And maybe it's forgivable since you've probably already done something bigger that helps her make a change. Hell, however it winds up with Greer, giving someone who needs a second chance a safe place to land is commendable."

I'm a guy and he's right about that last part even if I'm not thrilled to take credit for it. So I *whatever* my oldest friend and follow that up with "Gotta go."

Work is closed through New Year's Day, but I've got two active dogs to let out who are used to galloping at full speed in the wide space at the training center. They're being treated to Brighton's finest dog park today.

As I pull on my jacket Kimber stops to hug me before going around the bar.

"Thanks for delivering the soaps. They smell divine!" She pats my chest in a reassuring manner. "If you want dinner tomorrow there's a seat reserved at the table for you."

"You're welcome. And thanks. I'll consider it." I ought to accept on the spot, but don't. Spending the holiday barricaded at home with my mutts holds a certain appeal.

Chapter Ten

Greer

Nowadays, I'm totally sitting on the bed watching the living room TV when Byron gets home from work. I've felt like an interloper since getting back from my holiday with my mom and dad. I've fed myself sandwiches and been too busy to sit on the couch for a movie or hang out with Byron. Mostly because I push my chores off until the evenings so that there's no confusing the issue. Byron's not interested in me staying.

He offered me this room until I found something bett... er, uh... suitable for an ex-con. If I were a guy, not getting involved with anyone who'd killed her first hope of a committed relationship would be sort of a no-brainer too.

Not that a single kiss leads to walking down the aisle. I have more than enough experience with kisses leading in the opposite direction.

Unlike most weekdays, my hands are occupied and I can't flick the remote or casually close the bedroom door before the front door opens. The twisting motion has nothing to do with what they've done more times than I'm proud to admit the few nights Byron has cornered me to talk about the new batch of vets and dogs at the training center, or what's left the fridge, or thanking me for bleaching the tub grout in the hall bathroom. Or even wanting to discuss Jovie's reaction to Tallulah's adoption day, which for a dog used to having a companion has been what I'd figure a stint in solitary confinement is for a human.

Jovie trots into my room. She looks around longingly. Circling twice, she settles where Tallulah's dog bed had been, right on top of my current project, and sighs.

Poor girl. She is sure she's going to come back home at the end of the day and miraculously find her best friend here. I know exactly what that's like.

I finish the last stitch in the row, put my crochet hook down, and slide off the bed to sit next to her. Jovie's ears are silky soft. She shimmies toward me, asking for a belly rub, and a little bit of closeness.

"Jov, where did you… Oh." Byron stalls in the threshold. He raises a brow. "What's she laying on?"

"A bedroll."

"Smart. But I thought we discussed sleeping on the floor already?" Byron lowers himself to the plush carpet. Using the bed frame to brace his back, he tents his knees.

"Har-har. It's not for me. You can make sleeping mats by crocheting plastic bags together."

"Why would anyone ever do that?" He fiddles with the long line of plarn—plastic that it took me all of last week to cut and knot together to make yarn.

"That piece is for the handle. I found out when I was at my parents' that shelters provide the mats to the homeless. There are actually a lot of homeless vets who live on the side of Brighton where I used to." I leave out that Byron is a vet, hoping he's smart enough to piece that bit of information together on his own.

"Why are you doing it?" he asks, sounding skeptical.

"What else am I going to do?" I worry my lip. "Although, it takes a lot more bags than I counted on. I need about a hundred more for the ties and by then I'll have only made one mat out of over five hundred grocery sacks."

I've been petting Jovie, who is in desperate need of a friend, not paying much attention to Byron because he's not mine. Not really. The room grows quiet. There's an ambulance chaser advertising on the television in the background. I hate enduring lawyer commercials with their stupid flashing police lights and melodramatic pounding gavels. The constant negative reminder is the worst part of trying to escape into the TV set.

I look up and Byron's regarding me with a thoughtful expression. "Between the soaps as gifts, the way you run around at work, and keeping this place vacuumed, I don't think you spend enough time thinking about the things that make you happy."

"Soap makes me happy." I shrug. I mean bees and all the things I can make from bee byproducts.

Byron gets to his feet and leaves the room. I release a breath that's as long and miserable as Jovie's sigh when she understood Tallulah still wasn't in here. I wonder how long it will be before she gives up on looking for Tallulah in my room. If I were a dog, I wouldn't have lasted this long, but that's because I've had other experiences. I'm about to go back to crocheting when Byron jogs back, holding a small box of gloss.

"This is for you."

I reach out, shaking my head in confusion. Byron bought me a gift. We'd expressly agreed on no Christmas presents. But it's mid-January and... my stomach flip-flops the way it does when we've accidentally brushed by each other. Or Byron's talking to me. Or when I think of him and what I've done thinking about him in my bed.

"I ordered it while you were gone. When it came, I

chickened out on giving it to you to make the next batch of lip balm organic. Kissing you was—"

"A mistake. I get it. You don't need to explain and make it more awkward." I let the box drop to my lap, stroking the raised lettering that says there are multiple shades of dye inside.

"Greer, it was wrong of me not to ask you if it was okay."

"Because I had a girlfriend?"

"That. And I don't want you to think you're indebted to me the way Waylon tried to use you. It's a slippery slope, Greer. We work together and live together. I don't want you or anyone else getting the wrong impression." Byron loops a finger into mine, shaking our joined limbs.

His touch feels comical. And it feels heavenly. And it feels like yet another letdown. No one needs to get the wrong impression. I won't ruin a good man the way I destroyed the last boy who stole a piece of my heart.

Jovie's taken to Greer as a replacement for Tallulah. Little by little, instead of keeping Jov at my side to combat her loneliness, I've begun leaving her at home. Greer's early shift overlaps with mine. By the time I'm headed to work there are only a few hours that Jovie is on her own. It is good for a dog's independence, and having Greer's undivided attention—something Jovie had been seeking from me while I was trying to focus on getting the training center's latest bunch of recruits ship-shape—is working wonders as well.

Greer often has pink cheeks from tossing the ball out in the yard. She doesn't stay cooped up in her room nearly as much as she had in January. Jov sleeps soundly on the couch between us after dinner. I have intentionally accidentally brushed Greer's hand when we've both reached into the popcorn bowl. Last night, I slid her hips to the side in the kitchen, making light of Greer being in front of the microwave when it beeped. Her eyes widened with what I think was a spark of interest, and she flushed an even prettier rosy shade.

I want less space and more between us. I want to find out how warm that glow is underneath my fingertips. It burned me through the fabric of her worn jeans. I'm uncertain if I'm setting fire to the bridge we'd need to cross and deepening the gap that divides where we are from where I'd rather be.

I've never taken it so painfully slow with a woman. I act natural, not wanting to be the asshole that coaxes her into something she's not ready for and might never be. If there's an us then, there's no room for regret. However, I can't deny the pressure I put on myself to remain a gentleman, slowly showing her what she means to me, is breaking my resilience.

I'm dying a slow death and my skin is tight and chapped from the dry winter air and the number of showers I've taken. My dick aches from whacking off and alternately—when I feel guilty for masturbating over a woman who has impressive resolve—my balls ache for the imaginary feeling of emptying myself inside of her.

"Byron, would you mind bringing this to Greer?"

Karen surprises me from behind. I've been staring out the break room window at the dormant hives since the last class of the day got out.

I grunt, startled out of my own thoughts, and do a quick body scan before acknowledging the owner. I've gotten hard in the car in the afternoons, having to circle the block so that I don't walk in the house and scare Greer with the tent in my pants.

"Sure. What have you got?" I clear my throat and accept the bag. It pulls at my shoulder, heavier than I expect, piquing my curiosity.

"Five pounds of wax. Greer ran out making the last batch of soap and those cute little lip balm tins. Mac knows she won't come out and ask to replenish her supply. He had me pack up a bit of what's stored. Lord knows after a decade tending bees, Mac has more of it coming out of his ears than ear wax."

I chuckle at Karen's quip.

"Thanks, Greer will really like this."

Karen's right. Greer's soap making has been on hold. She has plenty of other ingredients, but no wax. That's why she started hoarding sacks and crocheting mats. When I purchased the gloss color kit, the cost of beeswax struck me. Greer wants to experiment with more than soap and lip balm, but she's not the type to put her wants first. It's why I try to do little things for her, like buying those lip balm tins. And why I'm glad Karen walked in here with overloaded arms to resupply Greer.

"I hope so. Anyhow, how is her search going? Has she found a new place to stay yet? Mac and I are still willing to take Greer on. It's no bother. She can stay as long as she likes. No buses to catch. The walk is shorter." Karen shakes her head, dispirited at Greer's aversion to accept a ride from her.

"She hasn't found a place yet." *Fuck if I let her.* "But I'll pass on the offer. She is a walker alright." *Don't push her on this.*

I recall Greer's statement that learning to drive is something she'll avoid at all costs. I respect her boundaries. Karen and Mac should too. Hell, I'm happy for the odd occasion Greer agrees to ride shotgun to the supermarket.

Then again, maybe I'm thankful for Mac pushing me to deliver Greer to her apartment when it rained. Yes, putting it that way makes it less like he was trying to wield control over Greer. The situation is tough. I hold Mac, Karen, and Greer in high regard. But my feelings for Greer are growing and I'm grateful the universe aligned and that she's safe with me instead of using a plarn sleeping mat on the streets.

"I got a call from Phil," Karen says, taking me off guard.

"Greer's last meeting with him is coming up." I bite down on the gum I can't stop chewing, nearly biting the inside of my cheek between my molars. I don't think the topic is appropriate between Karen and me.

"That one problem was the only problem. Now she's free to do what she wants."

I lick my lower lip, biting into it. The comment is a matter of perspective. Undoubtedly Greer sees it in a different light. She served her sentence. However, in terms of others' treatment of Greer over Ellis's death, she hasn't fully atoned for her sins.

Karen motions to the bag I'm holding. "There's a lot more for Greer at our house." Her tone leaves no room for confusion.

Karen wants Greer to move in.

But that's not where I want Greer. I don't live there and Greer's a full-grown woman, not an animal to re-home. So how do I convince Greer that I can make her as happy as the bees before becoming no more valuable to her than a drone that gets kicked out of the hive?

Chapter Eleven

Greer

Byron's army buddy, Trig, has been bringing Tallulah to the training center for a puppy play date every other week. I've lost a lot of people in my life. Some I'll never see again. So I hitch a ride for the chance to pet and cuddle her.

Jovie would tell you that dogs have feelings too. You can tell by how depressed Jovie was and how she seems to anticipate hanging out with her best gal pal. Tallulah's always excited to see me too, which reassures me she misses us the way we miss her.

Although, I'm certain she has a great family. Trig bought her special noise-canceling earphones. I thought it was over the top until I found out he brings her into a noisy bar a lot. Then when he put them on her to show off I thought it was adorable. Tallulah doesn't even bat a pat to get them off her head.

Kneeling in the dirt, I hold her muzzle and nuzzle her nose. "You must've practiced to keep these on, good girl."

She sits wagging her tail. It's Jovie who wants them gone.

Done with the demonstration, Trig pulls the muffs off and rewards Tallulah with a treat. It's not until he gives her a command that her bottom rises and Tallulah and Jovie spin around, herding each other in messy circles.

"Trig's wife is in charge at Sweet Caroline's." Byron fills me in.

"Not for much longer. She's giving her notice soon. We've kept it quiet that our son is about to become a big brother two times over. Byron here is the only person besides family we've mentioned the babies to so far." Trig readjusts the winter hat he wears rain or shine.

I congratulate Trig on his twins. My heat radiates inside my chest having him confide his secret in me. But who am I going to tell?

The weather is nice today. The guys intend to sit outside. I spy a six-pack in Trig's passenger seat. The brown bottles glint in the sunshine.

It's not as if we have zero alcohol in the house, but beer and cars bring out my inner turmoil. I make an excuse about finishing my cleaning and go back inside. Trig shows up on Saturdays or Sundays and I leave a few chores, like breaking down boxes and resupplying the paper towels in the restrooms to keep me busy because I actually do have two days off. Plus, Karen reminded me she doesn't care when it's done, it's that it's done. I've been trying to stay on her good side because she's been pushy about me moving in with them.

I appreciate their offer, but I need some breathing room. I can't deny Karen a connection to Ellis. But memories of Ellis are embedded into every nook and cranny in that house. It's only been the past few months that what I did to him doesn't weigh on my mind and invade my dreams.

You take her son. You take the beeswax. Yet you won't accept her hospitality? I admonish myself, placing industrial side rolls of TP on the stockroom shelf.

The closet closes in on me and I head for the break room. I take the spray disinfectant and a sponge and scrub every flat surface. When it's time to rinse, Trig's voice floats through the open window.

"So this kid who is dating Kimber's daughter and lives with us, Morgan. He did some time. For what the legal and probation system considers, he is reformed and he's going on to live the life of a model citizen. But what if another guy made a choice worse than Morgan's?"

"Like killing a man." Byron suggests.

"Indirectly. I mean, let's say he wasn't told by his commanding officer to point and shoot."

I cringe. Byron and I have talked about what separates our pasts, but sometimes—in my worst moments—I can't help wondering if he's blowing smoke. Acceptance of me is often tied to what I can do for someone else. Waylon wanted a blow job. Karen wants all of my memories of Ellis.

"I get it. For argument's sake." Byron's reply to Trig makes my stomach tense.

"The guy's done with that. He's moving on. But is there a point to his redemption if he goes on to live his best life for decades and he can still be incarcerated? If he still loses everything he's worked for while becoming more of an asset to society than a liability."

I shouldn't be listening to their private conversation. My own experience has been one you're deemed dangerous there's no before or after. There just is.

Chunks of my life stopped existing: Greer in kindergarten proudly showing her parents she'd written her name in wobbly orange crayon. Fourth grade Greer standing on her tiptoes to match Ellis's lanky height when we were the last contestants in the school spelling bee. Teenage Greer who'd fallen in love with her best friend. All those versions of me died alongside

Ellis. I'll forever be Greer at eighteen, charged as an adult, and missing the last promised weeks of my senior year and the life we could have led. My decision was stupid and arrogant and it defines people's reactions to me, including Byron's.

I've missed the last few exchanges, though Byron's position is clear.

"No matter what this guy chooses, if his wife looks anything like yours does, she isn't going to be lonely when he's sporting an orange jumpsuit."

I tear up as the pair throw jovial insults. Byron finds Trig's wife attractive. He's never called me beautiful. Our kiss was a mistake. He doesn't want anyone getting the wrong impression that he'd be attracted to me.

"I can't believe I gave my dog to a criminal," he says.

I drop the sponge in the sink and flee.

"I'm taking Karen and Mac up on the offer to move in." Greer stunned me by saying last night as she rinsed the popcorn bowl.

"Have you told Karen?" I thought she was happy here.

"Not yet."

"When did you decide this?"

"A while ago. I've tried not to crimp your style, but you probably want your bachelor pad back."

"I didn't ask you to stay out of my way, Greer." It came out defensive.

I'm as frustrated as I was when I gave her Karen's

excess beeswax and she didn't enthusiastically rush to test out the lotion recipe she found online, citing that there wasn't anyone to give it to and she was waiting until later in the spring to have Mother's Day gifts.

I leave her alone while she crochets and crafts because she's got an air of determination while she's doing them. Proud of the results, I gain a little of her attention, hoarding it the way she is those five pounds.

For Valentine's Day Greer decorated her bedroom with heart paper garland made from the pages of old books she picked up at the thrift shop. The hardbound cover became a mobile she suspended from the ceiling with honey bees flying out. I couldn't decide if the curling pages resembled leaves or teardrops. Either way, it was as stunning as she is. She'd traced the insects using the silicone candy molds as a pattern. Some extra sheets turned into a bouquet of calla lilies—again with a random bee on the petal—she's displayed on her dresser using an old spaghetti sauce jar she rinsed out and kept from dinner as a vase.

I'll tell you one thing, that woman isn't wasteful. And another thing, I hadn't a clue what a calla lily was until she told me. Then of course she launched into bees and pollen, the swarms in the hives becoming more active in the spring, and I sat and listened to her light up.

Bees make her happy.

I don't.

And knowing I don't makes me very unhappy.

I'm the fucking drone.

I wish I were as oblivious as they are because Greer leaves me in suspense, waiting to be kicked out of her life. The more patience I have for her, the more evenings I draw her out of her room so we can spend time together, less I have for anything else.

And the innocent bewildered look she gives me, when touching her now is wholly intentional on my part, makes me realize she's holding me at a distance.

"You got a minute?" Mac leans against the door jamb. He's eating an apple down to the core.

I shuffle a few things around my desk, letting out a deep breath. "Yeah, yeah…" The hammer is about to come down hard. "Listen, the vet today. I was curt with him. I know better. The dog and the guy are a good match."

"Not here to talk about that." He waves me off, getting comfortable in the seat. "Those soldiers have been to boot camp and had physical therapists ride their asses. We train people as much as we do the dogs. Maybe even more so. Sometimes it takes longer for the pair to click. If we have to make an adjustment down the road, it won't be the first time. The most even-tempered animal takes persistence and a good dose of humility to build a relationship with."

"So, why are you here?"

"Greer says she's moving in."

My jaw ticks.

"Ah, ha." Mac's scolding sounds a lot like "You don't want her to leave."

I unwrap another piece of gum and stuff it in my mouth.

"You know, Karen forgave Greer long before I found it in my heart to do so? It was Ellis that changed my mind. He was about fifteen the first time I saw it."

"What?"

"The way Ellis looked at Greer. She meant everything to him. He loved her. He probably loved her long before he ever realized it himself. He dated plenty to make the girl jealous.

"Greer made a horrible mistake. It's one she lives with because she looked at him the same way. She can't take back that one misstep, with no malice behind it, that ruined both their lives. Tore apart all our existences and stole every hope we had for their futures. I forgave Greer because that's what Ellis would have wanted me to do. That's the man I was trying to raise. If I intended to hold Ellis to that standard, it was high time I grew to it as well."

"I don't think anyone would have faulted you for having a different opinion than Karen." Not even Karen.

"Neither do I. But after we lost Ellis, my grief made the choice for me to also lose Greer. She was a girl whom I loved as much as a daughter because they'd grown up side-by-side. I began questioning, if she were my daughter, what my reaction would have been to her getting behind that wheel? Anger... hurt... despair... They were all there. But withholding love from my actual child? It wasn't an option."

Mac gets misty-eyed. "That happy little girl my son fell in love with while they were growing up was a full-fledged woman the next time I saw her. Greer broke down sobbing when she told me how sorry she was. She'd said the same words to me four years before. I simply wasn't ready to hear them."

Mac visited her in prison with Karen and Greer's mom. He re-established his friendship with Greer's dad, who had left Brighton when his business failed. He offered her the job here when no one would give Greer a chance. And when she took an interest in his hobby, he'd fostered her enthusiasm.

"I gave her those golden bricks of wax because nothing else made her happy. Cleaning up is not a purpose in life, Byron. And neither is moving into your former best friend's parents' house to atone for your guilt."

"Karen will be devastated. She wants Greer there."

"Don't fool yourself. Karen wants *Ellis* there. She gets a small piece of our boy back with every story Greer shares. Greer's still alive though, and none of us should be living in the past. Not if we can help it."

We stand at the same instant.

"Mac, I think I'm—" I'm compelled to confess. I'm

probably the last person he should trust to ask to change Greer's mind or inform her she isn't welcome on their doorstep.

"No." He holds up his palms. "No. The woman you care for deserves to hear you love her before you tell anyone else."

"How did you…"

"Don't you think after seeing it in my son that I can't recognize it in another man?"

"This may not be the happiest news to her. She might move in with you, anyway."

Mac's head bobs, measuring what I've said. "Well, if she does, you'll have a legitimate reason behind yelling at my vets then, won't you?"

Chapter Twelve

Greer

I've lived with Byron for five months. He's held out on having a social life other than an occasional drink with Trig. I'm sure if his friend's *gorgeous* wife is the manager at Sweet Caroline's she has plenty of women she can introduce him to. Being here has allowed me to save my pennies. Maybe my bank account will be flush after the same amount of time staying with Mac and Karen, and I'll be able to get ahead and afford a studio apartment on this side of Brighton. Maybe that's a pipe dream. All I do know is Byron has better things to do than babysit me. I'm holding him back.

I packed my bedroom into boxes today and used the ladder to reach the pots and pans stored in the garage rafters. In the kitchen, my hips sway back and forth, the music floating through my earbuds. The playlist had begun melancholy, but as the hour has worn on, it transformed into something upbeat. I mouth a few lines of lyrics, bending to reach into the cabinet where my soap making supplies are, planning to pack them next.

A brush of fingers at my waist gives me pause. If this had happened last fall I would have jumped out of my skin. A few years ago, I wouldn't have thought twice about turning and punching or slapping my assailant with a flat open fist. There is a familiarity of tenderness to it; a soothing warmth flowing from my hip down to my toes and back up toward my heart before settling into my core.

It's gone... And then Byron touches me again in the same spot.

"You're home early," I say a little too loud as I stand to put my double boiler on the countertop.

He looks at me. His Adam's apple bobs and I swallow reflexively as he removes a single bud from my ear and puts it in his own. His grip on my waist is still firm, and Byron tugs me closer, wrapping his arms around me.

He rests his head against mine as we rock to the uptempo music. It's one of those songs that isn't quite slow and yet it's a ballad you can't exactly cut a rug to. Ellis was my last dance partner and the clumsiness of the ballad makes me feel like I have two left feet.

But if I tripped, Byron wouldn't let me tumble to the floor. It's a sensation I've sought in the darkness when I skim my hands over my skin. It's the security I have when I stand under the bright streetlamp at daybreak waiting for the bus and realize I haven't had a bad dream while I've slept. And the reassurance when Byron shows up at work and again here at the end of the day.

I shouldn't be so tied to him. Dependent on his kindness. Considering making this man feel the way I feel about him is wrong. I don't know how to love. Just ask Ellis. I've never been able to commit to anyone. Just ask Ilona. And here Byron is dancing away with a heart I'm desperate to give him instead of having him steal.

His lips find the shell of my ear. My nipples harden. I pull away out of utter embarrassment before I rub them against his chest, seeking the slightest relief. But Byron's arms cinch me closer. I want to melt into him the way my body melts into the mattress, imagining his mouth on my breasts and his soft caress between my legs.

"Stay," he whispers.

My feet still. The remaining earbud falls. I search his face, positive I haven't heard him correctly.

"I don't have it in me to beg, Greer." One hand cups my cheek the way he did when he kissed me. The other laces through mine, squeezing. "Please, just stay. I swear I'll be a patient man if you do." He drops his forehead to mine as if his confession is painful.

"There's someone out there for you."

He steps back, grabbing the back of his neck and raking his fingers forward, messing up his hair. "There's someone right here for me. I fall a little bit more every day and if you go, it'll be like tumbling off a ledge."

"Fall. For me." It's supposed to be a question, but the incredulity in my voice is apparent. My rigid spine hits the counter. "You said kissing me was a mistake. And that working together was a problem."

"Because I didn't ask if it was what you wanted, and you said you don't have much experience, and I never wanted Mac and Karen to think that I'd use you the way Waylon tried to."

"I had a girlfriend."

"What do you want me to say to that? That it's a turn on? A turn off? That it's not in the back of my mind that I'm also shy of forty and making a goddamned fool of myself?"

"What I want is for you to acknowledge you're not the first person to kiss me. And that maybe I liked it. And that maybe you hurt my feelings by telling me it was a mistake!" I grow louder. Since I'm already making a spectacle out of myself, I go for broke. "And for fuck's sake, don't ask me to stay and then expect me to split the water bill for all the showers you take!"

Byron slumps into a kitchen chair. A lazy grin overtakes his smart mug. A throaty chuckle escapes him. He looks at me and I laugh at how awkward we are. I should be making goo-goo eyes at him for asking me to stay.

"You're so fucking beautiful when you blush. It's the first thing I noticed about you."

"It is not. I'm an ex-con and you're freaked you are harboring a criminal."

"When have I ever said that?"

"I overhead you telling Trig you couldn't believe you gave Tallulah to a criminal."

"That was a good-natured ribbing between old friends. I was only trying to lighten the mood, and he took it on the chin. Trig's got a guy working for him who is on parole, too. Morgan is younger than you, lives in their attic, and he dates Kimber's daughter. On top of giving the kid the second chance he deserves, Trig is working though his own personal bullshit. If I didn't think he could take the joke, I wouldn't have mocked him the way I did. But I'm also sorry that you overheard and it hurt your feelings. Can you accept my apology?"

Byron stretches a hand out to me, bridging the gap. I reach toward him, accepting what he's offering at face value since Byron hasn't gotten angry that I was eavesdropping. This time, the laugh he releases is a guarded chortle. I walk closer to him until our knees press together.

"Now that we've put that misunderstanding to rest, tell me how to convince you to stay," he pleads, placing a hand on my waist. His thumb makes small circles on my hip.

"For starters, stop holding back if it doesn't feel natural."

Byron guides me to straddle his lap. His thick, hard length punches up between my legs. "This is what you do to me, Greer. Hiding it so I'm not pressuring you is killing me. This is where I want you."

"Okay."

"That's it? I tell you I'm falling crazy in love with you and all I get is *Okay?*"

"Can you just stop talking and kiss me, Byron?" I brush my lips against his and use my tongue to part his lips. He doesn't hold back, falling over the edge and plundering my mouth.

Byron

Last night we kissed. Then we made dinner and sat on the couch with Jovie propping our popcorn bowl while we watched a movie. Greer gave me the side-eye sneaking Jov bites. I tossed a handful in her direction. Jovie went after every morsel, tipping the bowl and devouring what was left.

Greer laughed until I pinned her to the cushions and rocked my hips in unison with hers. Her smile faded as her lips parted and her tongue darted out of her mouth in an invitation to kiss her some more. The strangled moan that escaped her when she peaked turned me into a horny teenager, coming in my pants.

My boxers slicked to my stomach, I walked Greer to her room and leaned her against the door, intending on giving her a single goodnight kiss.

Jov trotted in behind us. She laid down on the mat over the spot that used to be Tallulah's, settling down for the night.

"Are you coming back to sleep in here too after you

clean up?" she winked saucily.

"Need someone to tuck you in, honey bee?"

"Or ward off the chill. Whichever you prefer." Her finger grazed the scruff on my chin.

I took the fastest fucking shower I've taken in months. Rifling through my drawers, I tossed on a looser pair of underwear that wouldn't strangle my dick and make the blatant erection that I haven't been able to get rid of less pressure for Greer. We can still take a slower pace.

"Byron," she said before sleep overtook us. "I like being here. I like being with you. But what if I don't know how to love you back?"

I can tell by the way Greer speaks about her parents, Karen and Mac that she's no stranger to love. I can see the adoration in her wide eyes when she's taken care of the pups. Greer has the propensity to love. But she's walled off her heart. "Maybe together you can learn how? Maybe you've forgotten?" *Maybe you're too scared right now, but I'll show you it's worthwhile,* I leave out. I have as much to lose as Greer does if our friendship isn't meant for this test.

In the morning, I drop my nose to Greer's neck, tugging her back to my front as she silences her alarm. Snuggling back into the sheets, Greer's warm palm rests on my ass. I snake my forearm up between her breasts over her nightshirt. It's short and there's a gap of silky skin showing above her panties. It's sexy, subtle, and inviting. Although once I'd gotten into her bed, all I did was hold Greer. I'm scared her fears will take over and she'll take off, anyway. All I can do is hope whatever this is will withstand the test.

"I have to go to work," she says.

I grunt in agreement, but don't move a muscle. Even when she's not making soap, Greer's hair smells like honey. I'll probably intrinsically associate the scent with her for the rest of my life.

"I don't want to go."

"Call in sick," I suggest, knowing full well Greer will refuse.

"I can't do that." She's never missed a day. That's not how a giver's brain functions.

"Then stay in bed for a while longer and I'll drive you."

"You don't have to be in until later. I can't ask that of you."

"Can't and won't are a matter of nuance. Like could and should. I should let you get ready so you don't miss the bus. But why, when I could bring you in myself and it would take less time?" I pause. "Are you more comfortable taking the bus than the car?"

"No. I've driven with you to the store plenty."

Assured it's her sense of responsibility, and not wanting to put anyone out, I tighten my hold on her.

"We're just going back to sleep until it's time to leave?" she questions, her butt wiggling into my groin. She moves my hand, sliding it underneath her top.

And I'm fucking awake.

Her nipples are hard points, and her waist undulates when I knead her breast. My lips press kisses to the base of her neck and my tongue follows, trailing to the soft spot behind her ear. We've been playing with her lush, firm tits together. She removes my hand by sliding it down her torso toward the elastic of her panties. When I hesitate going any further, it's Greer that slips our conjoined hands under the soft fabric. It's Greer that guides my hand to her pussy as the leg she isn't laying on splays over mine, granting me more access.

She moans with a shudder, placing the pad of my finger on her clit. She's so wet my first thoughts consist of burying my dick inside of her and how to make her come. And then she dips her own finger inside with a gasp of unadulterated pleasure. I get a coherent image of this woman lying in the bed touching herself the way

I've wanted to. I rub my cock against her ass, never having been harder for anyone.

I pluck her finger from her cunt and slide one of my own deep inside her channel. The blankets have rumpled at the bottom of the bed and her shirt has risen, exposing her tits. Greer goes back to playing with her breasts while I finger fuck her. The way she touches herself is the sexiest, most empowered thing ever.

She doesn't need me to please her. And me? I'm getting off watching her.

Greer turns her head and our lips connect. She opens wide for me; Her mouth and then her legs, giving me more access to the haven in between.

"Show me what you like. What to do," she says, holding onto the tightest of threads.

Her climax already building, she cries out at the loss when my finger leaves her body. I take Greer's hand from her tit and tuck it back into her underwear. Slicking her palm with the evidence of her arousal, I wrap Greer's fingertips around my throbbing cock.

My hips set a steady clip and Greer's strokes become confident. I've lifted my knee to give her access and her thighs have collapsed together. Her legs twist, seeking pressure. I roll her to her back and make her switch hands, which she does without skipping a beat. Taking my own place back where she most needs it, I offer a second finger, stretching her soaked and swollen core.

"You're so close," I grunt, not wanting to come before she does. "Play with yourself the way you wanted me to play with you when the shower was on."

Her sex-hazed eyes flash to mine with a keen knowledge and her lazy fingertip circles her clit, pressing down with exquisite pressure that has Greer panting with every ministration I make. She quakes and trembles and my balls tighten, cum shooting over her skin and sheets.

Greer

I stare at the bucket of sudsy water unable to look anywhere else. If I don't, someone will see me trying to hide my smile. I'm so hot under the collar that I'm sure I'm blushing. It makes my lip perk because Byron told me he notices when I do.

"You're so fucking beautiful…"

I blush deeper while his words loop between my ears like a love song on repeat.

This morning was… ah, a moment I'll never forget? Maybe because I haven't been with anyone in so long I'd forgotten how someone else's hands on my skin felt. Although, touching Byron at first was weird. I hadn't wanted to come off as clumsy or the kind of inexperienced that consumed me the first time I was intimate with anyone. I didn't want to be bad at fooling around when everything he was doing to me was perfect… And earth-shattering.

My core muscles tense and I realize my panties are all wet. All I can think about is bedtime tonight, and Byron only dropped me off two hours ago. It's shaping up to be one long day. He hadn't even had time to shower before hopping in the car. I have to wash my sheets when I get home.

Home. I sigh and a million happily buzzing bees launch themselves out of my throat. I have to drop the mop and go lean against the wall to get my belly to stop flip-flopping.

This is all just too good to be true. I would have settled for: Byron randomly complimenting Greer that she's pretty. Greer moves into Mac and Karen's house. Greer's heart goes pitter-pat whenever she sees Byron at the training center.

My goals aren't lofty anymore. I'd go as far as to say I've forgotten the ones I once had as a kid. At this stage, I'll gladly settle for a full belly and not drawing any criticism.

The door swings open and Karen enters.

"I'm sorry. I was taking a break."

"Are you kidding me? You're impeccable. There's going to be an unwritten rule that you cannot tidy up once you move in because my current housekeeper pales in comparison." Karen puts her hands on her hips. "I don't want to take advantage. I do want to talk to you about transferring your things between the houses."

"About that." I begin sheepishly. "I'm going to stay put at Byron's... for a while." I hedge when Karen's brow creases.

"I thought moving was best."

"That was... Byron and I had," I search for an explanation that satisfies Karen. "A disagreement."

"About what, sweetheart?" She rubs my arm sympathetically.

"Roommate stuff. It's hard to live with someone when you've been on your own. Dishes in the sink. Shoes... Shoes are *huge* when there are dogs. Sneakers are expensive and the next thing you know, the soles are chewed and you have to replace them. And there's never enough hot water."

My rapid over-explaining leaves Karen blinking. "Well, I hadn't expected to hear Jovie was a chewer."

"Tallulah." My head bounces on my neck.

It's as if I'm ten and lying to Karen about where Ellis got the strawberry taffy from that busted his palate expander.

Spoiler alert: it was me.

"We'd still love to have you. Our offer is always open. Let me know whenever you change your mind." My childhood best friend's mother is crestfallen. My own mentioned they'd discussed ways to decorate the spare room I was taking. I deferred to their ideas. After all, it's Karen's house.

"I appreciate that. It means—It means everything, Karen."

"So, have you melted the wax I sent over?"

"I'd been saving it, but Byron's army buddy and his wife are having a gender reveal party for their twins soon."

I'd been over the moon last night when Byron asked me to go with him. In all honesty, I hadn't a clue anyone celebrated the sex of their baby before it was born. However, we're supposed to bring gifts for the expectant parents instead of the babies. Byron saw a bunch of things at the bee shop that he's encouraging me to try out.

My enthusiasm slips out before I can catch it.

Karen winces. "Are you going to the party with Byron?"

"Yes ma'am. Because I've met Trig, and it's a chance to see Tallulah."

"That's lovely. I'm sure you'll have a wonderful time. Keep your shoes on, though."

"My shoes? Oh, yeah. I definitely will." *Oh, shit!* "Is there anything else you need, Karen? I can come over after lunch?" I was stopping at the thrift shop, but that can wait if she needs to talk about Ellis.

Karen pats my arm. "There are things I need to see to today. We'll get together soon."

Byron

"They're dating." Karen's shrill squeak is audible from the hall.

"It's not your business," Mac responds, even and calm.

"Everything about the business *is* our business."

"Um, hey. You wanted to see me?" I stand in the doorway. A horrible prickle travels up my back. Karen hadn't sounded off when my walkie crackled with the request to meet her in Mac's office after my session let out.

"Did you call Byron in here? Karen, leave it," Mac warns.

"I did because Byron let his temper get the best of him with the new recruits yesterday. Now that I know why, I'm unhappy he brought his personal problems to work."

Mac grabs Karen's shoulders, squaring them. "We do not have a policy against employees dating. I'm not about to enact one posthumously. And right now, you are letting your feelings cloud your concerns."

"I am not!" Karen shrugs him off.

"You didn't leave that kid hanging, did you, Byron?"

"No, sir." Mac had requested I work one-on-one with the vet who wasn't connecting with his dog. I've just finished up with them and they're confident in the intermediate commands now. But whatever I've done before answering Karen's request won't be enough. She's not mad at me about the vet. She's upset that Greer is staying with me.

"Then come on in and close the door." Mac motions me inside.

I do as I'm told because Greer doesn't deserve more people making her the topic of gossip.

Mac rounds his desk and looks out the window towards the hives. "It's important we're all on the same page. Byron and I talked this through already. He has nothing to apologize for. I gave him my blessing. I saw Greer this morning before she left for the day and, considering how happy she was, it's a safe bet they've discussed whatever their problems were in private."

"Why would you do that? Greer's a young, impressionable girl."

He turns, fisting his knuckles onto the desktop. "Because she has done everything to make amends with you. And the one thing none of us can fix is the past. Greer can keep feeding you all the things Ellis would never in a million years tell us because they were supposed to remain secrets between best friends, but it won't bring back what you lost. There's not going to be an Ellis and Greer. Our boy isn't here anymore."

"I can't believe you'd accuse me of thinking that. You and she spend entire afternoons out there with your metal steamy things, and nets over your heads."

"And we don't talk about anything except bees, Karen. I've gotten to know the Greer she is today. A woman who will stand in the dark waiting for a bus with a switchblade in her pocket to protect her. That Greer is as old in years as anyone in this office. She's not naive to the ugliness in the world, or susceptible to a man's unwanted advances."

"Ellis loved her." Karen chokes out. Her eyes, filled with tears, land on me.

"But for how long? How could we even know what Ellis and Greer could've had would last forever if they'd been sober? It's not fair to ask Greer to live her life in the past. We don't have an employee handbook and it's unreasonable to expect Byron to agree to us changing the rules on our whim."

"Well, I don't agree!" she shouts, storming out.

"Mac, I can—" Hell, I don't know what I can do besides give my notice. Greer certainly can't. Where else would she find a job surrounded by anyone who cares? "I'm sorry." My shoulders slump.

Mac huffs. "It's my own fault. I should have put a stop to it years ago, but she's my wife, Byron."

Mac hadn't wanted Karen hurt more than she was and staying silent kept them all victims of a terrible circumstance.

"Dealing with this won't be easy. On you. On Greer. I don't know if Karen will come around and see my perspective. I won't fight her if she doesn't."

I nod, agreeing with Mac because he has the objectivity from when Karen allowed him to make up his own mind about him seeing Greer when he was ready.

I'm on edge the rest of the afternoon. The feeling like my job is slipping out from under my feet keeps me on high alert. I'm kind to a fault with the former soldiers on the premises for training. I stay later, walking men and women, who are still slowly getting used to managing new lives with their prosthetics, and their dogs back through drills until they're secure with what I'm teaching them.

From the instant Karen and Mac approached me, they've been like a surrogate set of parents. Good people I depend on to help me see the good in others, and maybe even in me. Because even if your wounds aren't visible, there isn't a soldier I've met who has come back from a tour unscathed. If they could forgive

Greer, then I should eventually find it in my heart to forgive my wrong-doings.

Taking the long way through Brighton, I circle the block that Greer lived on behind Sweet Caroline's. The radio blares loud, angry music. I want to scream my motherfucking head off over it. It's not fair that life was perfect for only a few golden hours.

If I had Jovie in the car she'd need those noise-canceling earmuffs Trig bought Tallulah. I leave her home so often now because Greer is there. I don't even have to be stealthy about it. Jov has what I feared she'd lose when her companion moved on. Somewhere deep down I've found out something I was afraid to admit too: Jovie is getting older. She won't be around perpetually. And, when she's gone, I'll have no one.

As tough as it is, I guess that's why I can accept Mac's point of view about Karen. Without her, he has no one left either.

Greer

Byron's crossover pulls into the driveway as I'm modeling a new dress in the hall bathroom mirror. Its pattern is flirty, and it's probably way too short. It's definitely not something I can wear while cleaning. If I bend over I have to be careful my butt won't show. I justified the buy because I have a little padding in my bank account. The top also was such that it didn't require the padding of a new bra. Plus, I can get away with wearing the canvas sneakers I wore last summer if I run them through a bleach cycle in the washer.

I guess hearing Byron tell me he thinks I'm attractive makes me want to be attractive to him. Admittedly, it's not that I hadn't tried with the red sweater all those months back while my inner monolog stiffly maintained that it was just me dressing appropriately for the occasion. I suppose the part of me that's giddy over Byron's invitation agrees looking nice at the party is important.

Which is to say, I had a whopper of a mental argument on the appropriateness of rewarding myself with a twelve-dollar garment someone else has already worn.

Telling Karen today that I wasn't moving in was hard. But I'm proud that I did it. It won't be as tricky the next time. I'll have more confidence. I won't feel like I'm letting her down by sharing the things I remember about Ellis with her less frequently.

About to duck into my room and slip into my comfy jeans, a gruff grunt sends my shoulders to my ears and my bare feet skidding to a halt.

"Stop," Byron says in the same gravely manner as he'd asked me to touch myself this morning in bed.

An electric skitter of awareness prickles over my skin. I turn around before he commands me to. And make no doubt, those are the next words out of him.

"I've never seen you dressed up." Tossing his keys on the nearest hard surface, he swaggers toward me, pressing his body to mine. "I want a chance to admire you."

"You can't exactly look at me when I'm pinned to the wall, can you?" I smart, flushing.

We've changed course and are at a place where flirty interactions have been replaced with intimate, straightforward, and outright suggestive communication.

"Sure I can," he taunts, taking a lock of my blonde hair between his fingers and arching a brow.

"Speedycuts." I treated myself to a trim to get rid of the split ends.

With a wolfish grin, he brushes the lock over my back and places a kiss on my mouth. One more on my chin. A third, when my head shifts, exposing my neck, landing under my ear. His fingers dip between my breasts, cupping one and folding the layers of fabric down so that it's exposed to the air. Taking it between his lips, there's a tug from his teeth. Remnants of the shimmery peppermint lip balm I'd tested out tickle my nipple. A soothing pull follows as Byron sucks the slightest hint of pain away. Recognition that he intends on playing with my body again shoots right to my core, filling me with an aching need for the satisfaction he gave me when we woke.

I whimper as Byron's hand skids up my thigh, bunching the fabric to reach underneath the skirt, and drawing my panties down my legs.

He kneels. "Step out, Beautiful."

I lift my toes, doing as he says. He grasps my thigh, guiding it over his shoulder, and brings his nose to my pussy. A tentative tongue darts to taste me. My knees buckle and Byron's chest rumbles.

"You like that, honey bee?"

I hum my appreciation. The briefest pause in what he's doing causes my breath to come in sharp pants.

He slides his tongue against my slit again, curling it at the contours of my clit, and taking the hard nub into his mouth to suckle the way he had my nipple.

My shameless moans have Byron taking the weight of my hips. He grips my ass, bluntly instructing me to fuck his face. As if there was any question. I run my hand behind his neck. My fingers thread into his hair. The scruff of his perpetual five o'clock shadow combines with my titillating wetness. The two sensations create a third even more gratifying one. Two fingers enter my soaked cunt and my muscles convulse, tipping me over the edge, and making me cry out.

Steadying me, Byron stands and picks me up. He carries me to my bed, where he places me down. Without wiping the taste of me away, our tongues tangle leisurely while he readjusts my dress. The panties are still in the living room. Jovie is sacked out on my floor.

I cover my face. "Did she watch us?"

"No, she didn't. There's a reason she has a dog bed and doesn't sleep in mine."

"Ooh," I drag the syllables out. It makes sense that

Byron's had women over before, even if he hasn't since I've lived under this roof.

"I have a sticky question. Did you ever mention Ilona to Karen?"

"No."

Bisexuality played the smallest of roles. My parents accepted me for who I am. They'd taught me if anyone took issue with my sex life that was their problem, not mine.

Given the heat, we had much bigger fish to fry. I was already dealing with the judgment of others. Karen's and Mac's being the harshest. It was a conscientious decision to avoid the fact that while I'd wanted Ellis as a boyfriend, Ilona *was* my girlfriend. I never brought our relationship up with them because—male or female—I wouldn't have been as cruel during their brief visits as to make Karen and Mac believe I wasn't mourning Ellis anymore.

Karen has always needed that continued closeness to her son, and I was the only one who could give it to her. She once mentioned his aunt had become a grandmother. I wasn't rubbing her nose in the mud that —albeit a long shot—I still have the option of providing grandkids to my parents, but I'd taken that milestone from her.

"They've both figured it out, and she has a problem with us, Greer. A big one."

The knots in my belly while I'm working aren't as romantic as they'd been a few days ago. I slink around corners upon hearing Karen's voice, not wanting to answer questions about Byron. I don't want to lie to her about my feelings for him or the subtle moments when my heart considers where all of this is leading with him.

Part of me wishes I'd been more upfront about Ilona with my best friend's mother. If Karen was aware of another relationship, perhaps we'd have a starting point and whatever is happening now wouldn't seem strange and foreign. But I've also always known Karen's continued interest in me circled around my connection to Ellis. She's still working through everything she lost.

Aside from the potential future I'd stolen from all of us, I'd been afraid after Ellis died that I'd never get over having him as a confidant. How many people's first loves die, let alone at their hands? Not many, I'd predict. Ilona changed that. Although it's been almost as many years since Ilona's and my last non-goodbye, Byron's helped me wade through the waters and see I can let go of some of the hardest parts while holding onto the best memories.

I'm glad to have a friend in him. That Byron held me close, and we talked about our troubles when it was clear any relationship we have won't be smooth sailing. That he didn't use, abuse, and discard me after getting his way. Well, sort of his way. When I wouldn't give in to Waylon, he set out to teach me a lesson. But what I learned was there is someone I can depend on and who won't push me into anything I'm not ready for.

I'm also thankful for Mac's support. He's sought me out as I've hidden in the supply closet and placed a reassuring hand on my shoulder to talk with me about splitting the last hive he'd left whole a spring ago. Like his attitude about Ellis, never once has Mac pressed for information about where Byron and I stand. It makes it easier to acknowledge random things that have happened at home that Mac would find humorous, like Jovie's current infatuation with popcorn and how we can get her to do almost any trick for it. And not quite as awkward when I do mention Ellis's name in passing. We both do bring him up. We both miss him. But somehow we've bridged the gap from where we stood almost a decade ago and I'm thankful for that.

In Mac's presence, I worry less about retribution and either Byron or I losing our jobs. It was an enormous concern when Byron told me Karen was unhappy. It wouldn't take long for her to hire a new custodian. Mac has trained enough animal trainers over the years. Byron is replaceable. I'd have guilt if Karen fired Byron, or forced him to quit. He loves the training center. He has friends in Brighton and, like Mac and Karen have become, Trig is the only family he's got.

I fidget in the car on the way to the gender reveal, smoothing my dress and wringing my hands. Driving short distances with Byron has become as normal as riding the bus. I still prefer the bus. Statistically, there's a tenfold less likelihood of a crash and most car accidents happen close to home.

"Nervous?"

"That I'll make a good impression, yeah."

My mind wanders back to Byron's comment about Trig's wife being attractive. I've tried to block out him teasing Trig that he'd given Tallulah to a criminal. We wouldn't be going to this party if Byron really felt blindsided by whatever Trig is involved in, would we? I hope it's the case that he sees beyond my past and judges the full picture as well.

Please don't make today turn into a mistake, I silently plead as we pull up to the curb.

A small group of men are out front. A preschooler is on Trig's shoulders. He's wearing Trig's toque and tapping out the beat from the music, using the top of Trig's head as a drum. Two elementary school-aged kids are drawing with sidewalk chalk. We're introduced around—a few of the guys telling Byron it's nice to see him again—and make our way inside.

Hardly inside the door, Kimber greets us, motioning us to the kitchen. I gingerly place our gift on the counter and take a seat. Byron stands behind me.

"You've not once brought a guest, so... Scram," Kimber says polite but firmly, fluffing her fingers in his direction. To me, she directs a welcoming smile and offers me a choice of pink lemonade or baby blue punch. A stork-topped toothpick nesting on two maraschino cherries garnishes both glasses.

"Oh, I don't drink alcohol."

"It's okay. Neither do I—even when I'm not baking babies."

"Kimber concocts the best mocktails." A gorgeous blonde with victory rolls and bright red lipstick sitting next to me adds. "She taught me all of her secret recipes before she quit tending bar so that I could keep the Sweet Caroline's crew placated. A person could get stumbling drunk ordering one after the next... *if* they didn't know they were non-alcoholic. For the most part though, we just wind up on a sugar high and constantly peeing. I'm Holly by the way." She shakes my hand.

"Speaking of sugar highs and peeing, I passed my glucose test!"

"Go you!" Holly high-fives Kimber. "I would have been mightily concerned for Trig's well-being if you were off caffeine and chocolate croissants indefinitely."

"Right? Aidy brought me a whole bag from Baked Beans to celebrate. Aidy is my daughter." Kimber points outside to a college aged-woman with violet hair. The girl turns her profile at the same moment and I'm struck by how much more like sisters they appear than parent and child.

I glance back, and Kimber is rubbing her belly in slow circles.

"Are you excited that you may have another girl?"

"It doesn't matter to me either way. I'm simply glad to be doing this one last time and that Aidy is here to be a part of it. Our son, Owen, doesn't remember what it's like not having his big sister living with us. I can't imagine what O's life would be without her or Morgan. We're really blessed that they're around."

So this kid who is dating Kimber's daughter and lives with us, Morgan. He did some time.

That's what Trig said at the start of the Kimber-is-hotter-than-Greer conversation. And no doubt about it, even this far along with twins, Kimber holds a certain appeal I can appreciate. But I have Byron's attention and he has mine. And more than that, I don't quite feel out of place in suburbia. Or, like my outcast status, is anything Kimber is scrutinizing.

Chapter Fifteen

Byron

When Kimber booted me from the kitchen, I beelined for the backyard, figuring I'd see Tallulah out there. When I bent to pat her, she knocked me on my ass. As I got to my knees, she began searching for Jovie. Half feeling remorse that I hadn't brought her along, I did what any self-respecting dog lover would. I picked her up, took her back to the kitchen, and plopped all forty-plus pounds of her on Greer's lap.

Tallulah washed Greer's face in puppy kisses while Greer cooed to her. Then, exuberant over having her own important guests, Tallulah got excited, and we had to send her back outside to run off the zoomies that have Trig's preschooler—now pumping on the swings with the older kids we'd seen—laughing all over himself.

"Are you having a good time?" I check in case we need to make a quick escape.

We're washing our hands in the washroom. Kimber offered her a facecloth and gave us privacy so Greer could freshen up.

"These women are so pretty. And so nice." There is

bewilderment in her voice.

"See, you fit right in." I touch my lips to her nose.

As we reenter the kitchen, Kimber is wadding and shoving plastic sacks behind a canister.

"Can I possibly have those?" Greer asks.

"Um, sure." A curious Kimber watches Greer retake the spot she'd vacated at the counter to flatten and fold the bags.

"She weaves bedrolls with them for homeless vets," I supply when Trig's wife gives me an odd look.

Kimber scoots around the counter, squeezing my woman into a vise-like hug. "Oh my God, can we keep her, Trig?"

"Keep who? Greer? Nope, if that big belly you're toting around hasn't cued you in, My Love, we're about to have a full house. Plus, we took Tallulah and by the end you know he was dragging his feet about giving up the dog. Greer is Byron's."

I snort. His argument has teeth to it.

"You are bringing her back," Kimber commands.

I walk behind Greer and set my palms on her shoulders. "I will."

Sloan, Kimber's partner in crime, lifts a glass jar from the gift basket we brought and unscrews the lid. "This smells divine." Sloan breathes in deeply.

"It's beard oil with honey, and sandalwood and citrus extracts," Greer's hasty reply covers her skittish stutter.

She went to town building a basket filled with creature comforts; spa-quality lotions and soaps, eucalyptus shower steamers and bath bombs, beard oil and belly butter, which has something to do with stretch marks. Each afternoon, she'd been bursting with excitement to show me the next concoction. I'd gotten high on her buzz and we'd taken an impromptu ride to the store to find missing ingredients one evening. Although, as she packed everything into the basket, the concern Greer had that the gift wasn't up to snuff was evident.

"Oh my gosh, are you the one who made all the soaps and lip balms for Christmas?" Sloan exclaims.

Greer blushes, nodding and shrinking a little in her seat, uncomfortable with the attention. "I put some shower jellies in there for Owen, Kimber, so he felt included, too. They're in the shape of gummy bears. I just make sure he doesn't put them in his mouth because they don't taste quite as sweet as the real thing." Greer fidgets, sticking out her tongue.

"Can I get one of these for my son? Maybe he'll actually wash if he thinks he's getting sticky and dirty instead." Holly nudges Cece, whom I've met before. Her boyfriend is the handyman I would have insisted Greer call if she stayed in that shit hole apartment.

Cece takes the cellophane bag that looks like oversized gummy candy from Holly and requests jelly bears for her boyfriend's daughter and Holly's niece.

"Sure. I have extras I don't know what to do with."

"I need to tack on some lip balm because both little girls took what I had. Can I text you? And I can totally pay you now if you give me your Venmo."

"What's a Venmo?" Greer mouths, mystified. She's given Cece her cell number.

"Don't get flustered. We'll get you set up with one." I whisper in her ear.

Having met Kimber's girlfriends before, I'm not as surprised by their eagerness to support Greer.

Everyone is sniffing and sampling. Kimber has splashed beard oil in her palm and is patting Trig's jawline. Sloan asks if Greer can make the same scented bar soap.

"Do you know who'd love all of this? Paisley! Her boutique stocks the neatest stuff by her register. Paisley is big on sourcing items locally. I have her card with me." Sloan is about to dash off for her purse.

"I got you, girl," Cece calls. Her thumbs fly over the

screen on her phone and Greer's dings with multiple incoming messages, including the link to Paisley's website.

"What is going on?" Aidy's voice pushes through the ruckus and ping of enthusiastic messages that have Greer's phone screen scrolling with orders.

"Smell this." Holly holds the bottle of beard oil under Aidy's nose.

"Oh my gosh, I'd eat Morgan if he had this on."

"Right? It's manly and edible."

"Speaking of, if we don't have lunch soon, then we won't get to cut the cake. And if we don't cut the cake, the gender reveal will be at the hospital when the babies are born."

"I can't wait that long!" Kimber tosses up her hands in surrender. "I want to know. Either way, I don't care, but I have to be prepared!"

Trig tucks her under his arm, patting her back and kissing the top of her fiery redhead.

The kitchen empties with the other women carrying dishes and platters outside to the barbecue and picnic tables set up in the yard.

Dumbfounded, Greer peers up at me. "What just happened?"

"You got your first customers, honey bee."

"I'm shaking." She shows me her jittery hand.

I lace my fingers into it and bring our joined fist to my lips. "And I'm so proud of you."

"Where do you source the beeswax from?"

Byron and I have finished our loaded plates. Morgan and Aidy have seated themselves at the same long picnic table we are. A few others they seem to know well are here, too. However, Morgan's taken a genuine interest in soap making.

I like him. I'm not sure if it is because Morgan is soft spoken or that we have a weird connection having both been to prison. I mean, it isn't as if either of us have asked for the other's OPUS number or compared the shitty prison food. It's just like Morgan knows about my past and doesn't care and I know about his and I don't either. Actually, it's as if no one here cares to judge us. Surrounded by this group is the most normalcy I've felt.

"My boss is a beekeeper. He's been showing me how to care for the hives."

"How long has he done that?" Morgan folds and unfolds the original corrugated wrapper I'd put the soap for Trig inside of.

The bar is making its rounds at another table. People are *oohing* and *aahing* over it while I try to keep my head out of the clouds.

"Going on nine years," Unexpectedly, the constant weighty need to confess that Mac took up the hobby when Ellis died seems less significant. "We have a hive that's about to swarm, so we'll be splitting it soon."

"*How* do you do that?" Aidy interjects.

"Very carefully," I say, inciting a laugh. It's gotten easier to talk than when the questions were rapid fire in the kitchen.

"You put on those big white alien invasion suits?" Morgan turns to Byron.

"Don't look at me, man. I'm team canine. I don't think they have trainers for bee circuses, only flea circuses." Byron gives me a toothy grin, chomping on his gum with a loose jaw.

"Yes, we use protective gear and a smoker to subdue the bees."

"How many bees are in a hive? Aren't you worried about getting stung? I got stung when I was a kid. It's not something I'd volunteer to repeat." Aidy clutches Morgan's bicep.

"Thousands. I've been stung before too, but not recently. It's an occupational hazard." I don't see not getting stung as realistic.

"That's sort of kick-ass that you aren't afraid." Aidy compliments me as if I'm wearing Wonder Woman's tiara.

I want to tell her there are other things I lie awake worrying about. We've just met, so I keep it upbeat. Besides, I'm having a really good time surrounded by Byron, and Trig and Kimber's friends.

Everyone is vivacious. I never would have guessed Kimber—pregnant and chasing a preschooler to stop him from chasing Tallulah to feed her what's left of his spare rib—was as old as Byron. Apparently, so is Holly. The woman with victory rolls and the pin-up girl dress. Yet, a lot of the other women here are closer to my age or younger. And the men run the gamut too.

Other than Byron, I interact mostly with my parents and Mac and Karen. They seem so old in comparison. It must be what we've been through that's jaded my perspective.

"Hey O," Aidy snags her baby brother's attention. "Can you finish eating that rib so we can all have cake?"

"Dhere's cake?" his toddler lisp makes him sound like a drunken sailor.

Aidy points to a double-decker. The top round tier is slightly smaller than the bottom. The ombre frosting swirls from shades of light pink to turquoise. The baker has piped the most adorable sayings in icing like *Beard or Bow?, Mustaches or Eyelashes?,* and my personal favorite, *Cupcake or Studmuffin?*

Owen doesn't need to be told twice. He immediately nibbles the rest of the meat.

Kimber comes to a standstill next to her son. She places one hand on her lower back, relieved, and ruffles another into his already messy hair. Her expression, glancing between her two children, is utter joy and thankfulness.

Kids aren't part of the package for me. But what I wouldn't give for an ounce of the happiness Kimber feels.

Morgan swoops in to scoop Owen up and Aidy excuses herself to wet a napkin for the little boy's face.

Byron slips his arm around me. "You're smiling," he says low enough no one else will hear. "I caught you."

"Look at her. She's surrounded by support. She's so lucky."

"I'd rather watch you." He places a kiss on my collarbone where the skin peeks out from my dress. "Take a step back, Greer. All these women are supporting you. There are people who love you, too." Byron reminds me he is one of them.

Thank you. The response is reflexive.

The words *I love you* are on the trip of my tongue. They swell inside of me, building to a point that the overwhelming emotion gets trapped in my throat. I wasn't ready to say them to Byron just now and am not sure I ever will be. Risking my heart again is foolhardy. It isn't even fear that he'll change his mind and not love me back. I can't love someone and lose them again. Keeping that emotion bottled up stops the universe from serving up retribution for even attempting to love.

Yet there's an ache to staying silent. Creases wrinkle Byron's forehead. I cup his cheek, running my fingertips against the stubble. The golden light in his eyes dims, betraying his sorrow. I touch my lips to his in sweet benediction.

I wish I could spit out what he needs to hear with an

air of nonchalance that falls on fate's deaf ears. But that bitch listens. And I'm not ready to let him go and it's inevitable the better things get, the worse it's going to hurt when that happens.

A commotion near the rear of the house has everyone turning their heads. Scads of tiny blue M&Ms scatter onto the cement pad where the cake table rests. Owen chases the candy, squashing the shells under his shoes. He reaches out with frosting-covered hands, popping them into his mouth.

"Yummy!"

"Owen, no!" Aidy yells.

He's ripped the side off of the cake, spilling the proverbial beans.

"Trig, they're blue. All of the candies falling out at the bottom are blue!" Kimber grabs her husband by the collar.

"Hell, yes!" he bellows, taking a handful of cake for himself, and then offers Kimber a sticky lick from his finger.

She's beaming when Trig shout-announces the babies' names are Finn and Kennan.

"Is the top layer different?" Aidy's scooping up M&M's, trying to stop O from eating them off the ground.

"No!" Kimber shrieks, excitedly hugging her adult daughter. "Owen made a mess when he snatched a bite. The side of the cake is gone. It's two boys!"

Chapter Sixteen

Byron

Here's the thing: I've never thought much about having kids. I'm an only child raised alongside a barn full of animals. If I got lonely, a goat, or flock of chickens were there to listen to my troubles and horse around with. My parents were great. I didn't lack for attention or affection. I didn't lack for a damn thing until they passed on and I was left with their property and the proceeds from their life insurance. It was then I recognized stuff doesn't make up for people.

I had great people in my life while I was in the Army. I still do. And I'm fine with being a *Doggy Daddy* in perpetuity. I freaking flew Jovie across the globe for the chance to take care of her and it has meant the world to me.

But there was a split second at Trig's when I got a glimpse of how sweet his life is. It makes perfect sense now why he has doubts about certain activities he's involved in. Ones I choose to turn a blind eye to because of his surveillance business. I've heard plenty of rumors around Brighton that the owner of Sweet Caroline's—a guy Trig associates with—isn't on the up and up. I don't have near as much to lose. Yet, what I have isn't inconsequential, and I'd do anything to keep it too.

All I can think about this week is how to have my cake and eat it too. I refuse to forfeit my job because of my relationship with Greer. I won't give up on Greer when we're good together.

I'm not getting down on one knee with a ring. Or asking for the two-point-whatever children. Although if she'd say something—*anything besides thanking me*—when I tell her I love her, I'd paint the backyard fence white... Lay a blanket down on the grass outside... Pitch a few balls to our dog and let Jovie run with her tongue hanging out of her mouth... Recline next to Greer, watching the clouds float by, and know in my soul there were endless possibilities for us.

For a woman who isn't used to crowds and who hides from attention, Greer was impeccable at the party. The interest in her soap making and the orders the mill girls placed had her flying high by the time we'd gotten home. That night before bed, she was a whole new woman, flush with bold anticipation instead of apprehension.

In bed, she was as undaunted as ever. Greer's newfound confidence propelled her usual lack of shame about her body to decide to take me in her mouth. Flicking her tongue to taste the pre-cum at the tip of my dick, licking down my shaft, and hollowing her cheeks as she sucked me dry. I hovered above her, my fingers in her tight hot pussy and my lips savoring the sweetness of her sex.

Satiated, I'd held her close, dragging my fingertips over her upper arm while Greer traced the ridges of my chest. It was only then that her insecurities bubbled to the surface, beginning with not wanting to ruin any of the orders she'd received and ending with her admitting she's not ready for us to make love.

"I'm not on the pill. I only know what a condom looks like unrolled because I saw a used one in the gutter outside of my old apartment." Her nose wrinkled.

I rolled on top of her, rocking my hips against her core. The cotton of my boxers and her panties rubbed together created friction.

"There's no rush." I reminded her. What we'd done, her short nails scraping my balls while I swirled my tongue around her clit, was fine by me. And for as long as it had been since I dry humped a girl, so was what we were doing. "And there's nobody but you. You're safe with me."

Similar to the time it took for Greer to work her way from one concern to opening up about what was really on her mind, she deserves for her first time to be on her terms.

The following day we both had off, but Mac picked up Greer at lunchtime. The hives are active and if they didn't split the hives in a hurry, the bees would swarm. Greer was only gone for four hours, but they were the longest of my life. My head throbbed the way it does after too many beers and yet my misery hadn't a damn thing to do with drinking. I kept my misgivings that a hive would tumble, crashing open, and the propensity of the bees getting pissed to myself. I hadn't wanted Greer to leave doubting that this was something she was capable of.

After they moved the newly split hive to a different location, Mac brought Greer back.

"Glad to see you're still in one piece." I kissed her hello as soon as the front door shut.

"Oh, I'd still be in one piece if I got stung. I'd just have holes in me like a sieve." She waved off my apprehension with a gorgeous smile and satisfied laugh.

So the last thing I thought would happen this week was that the walkie hooked on my belt would cheep with a shrill squeal.

"I need an ambulance and an EpiPen out by the hives." Mac asserts with no preamble. "Now!"

"I've got the pen!" I hear banging and Karen's sneakers squealing on the linoleum as she dashes for the first aid kit.

I press my thumb against the walkie button. "Calling 911."

My heart thuds in my chest telling the operator exactly what I know. If someone needs epinephrine out by the hives, then they've been stung. And if Mac was the one shouting into the two-way radio, then it has to be Greer.

Greer

When I leave work Byron tends to be in the middle of teaching a class. I duck out, so as not to bother him. We'll meet up at home. And we're both in agreement that calling as little attention to our relationship as possible is for the best. Neither of us wants to be on Karen's bad side.

Yesterday, she'd asked me about splitting the hives. It felt good to have a normal conversation with her. I was so excited about Mac including me in the process this year. Plus, the ladies I'd met at the party are still texting me—something that's unbelievable to someone like me, who keeps to herself. I overindulged in telling Karen about the orders, how nice Byron's friends are, and how proud I am of myself alluding to how Byron is of me too. I talked to Karen like she was my mom, forgetting that she's Ellis's. Absentminded as to what I owe her. Of course, Karen reminded me she thought Byron was too old and using me and that I was better off living someplace else. Namely, her house.

Today, I stumbled into Byron completely by accident in the back hallway near the break room. Lost in his megawatt smile, the way the sunlight from the window highlighted those gold flecks in his scruff, I dared to sneak a kiss goodbye when no one was looking.

I didn't *want* Karen to catch us. Contemplating her reaction actually had me on high alert until I thought it through. I'm tired of being on pins and needles that the slightest indiscretion will have her up in arms. Or that the tiniest infraction might seal Byron's fate, allowing Karen to convince Mac that Byron shouldn't be a trainer here anymore.

Work was easy and life was hard before the holidays. Now, with the stress Karen is causing, that has reversed. I can't voice aloud that I'm worried about the underlying pressure it puts on Byron and me at home. What I want is for the weight of expectations to even out. Just a little. I mean, I am so far past looking for perfection it's in the rearview mirror. However, I'm finding it harder to believe the happiness Byron's brought to my life isn't doomed for destruction.

And believe me, I have had the moment where Karen's actions are justified, and I've wondered if losing Byron is my recompense. An eye for an eye. I took the most valuable thing Karen had from her. Why should she not do the same to me?

I do my best thinking while I walk. So I extend my hike to the bus stop with an impromptu trek across the field over to the hives.

Fundamentally, I know that I've given Karen as much of Ellis back as I have to give. Each time she needs me to, I rip at the shreds of my heart that have been woven back together, offering the frayed memories to patch the hole I left in hers. Except, the love I feel deep down for Byron means I'm healing. I've earned the right to let go of my past because I hadn't shied away from learning a valuable lesson. Maybe it's time to stop tearing myself up over this?

I'm glad for the sunshine. Earlier, my legs had been chilly in the denim capris I'm wearing. It's warmed up significantly as the morning has worn on. Long grass tickles my ankles as I stand at what I rationalize is a safe distance. I won't venture too close without protective gear, but the spring air, the buds unfurling new green leaves on the oak tree, and the outlying hum of the worker bees bring me a sense of peace.

I lift my knee, intending to brush the blade of grass scratching my heel and that's when I feel the sharp, fiery burn. Although I haven't been stung since I was a kid, my mind associates the pain in an instant. Adrenaline pumps through my veins. I've been waiting for this, but figured if it happened, it would happen while tending the hives.

Wincing when I put my foot to the ground, I turn to hobble back to the training center for sodium bicarbonate to relieve the sting and a bandage. Mac is coming out the back door, approaching me. I wave to him with a shaking hand and a tingling sensation starts at the base of my neck. The prickles wash up over my head, blurring my vision. Beads of sweat dampen my armpits as my knees go rubbery. My eyesight is like focusing through a pinhole camera. Mac is running toward me now. Then everything fades to black.

"Greer!" Byron yells.

There's a thick fog between my ears.

Gasping, I wake with a jolt. I'm lying on the ground. Mac's thumb is on the tip of a yellow auto-injector, his grip tightly wound around the plastic shell. I roll my head, feeling nauseous. There's a second, empty tube next to me and my leg aches with the ferocity of being sliced by a knife.

I rub my thigh, feeling for blood. Yet, all I come back with is an idea of where the hole the needle made in my pants is.

Karen has the back of her hand to her face. She's crying. Byron's still calling my name. Mac's telling them I'm alive. I don't remember dying. I don't remember anything at all until the paramedics arrive and I hear the words *bee sting*.

And about then—while the medics are scraping me to a stretcher and Byron lets go of my fingers—I wish my stupidity had killed me.

Chapter Seventeen

Byron

"You're lucky your boss saw you collapse." The ER doctor tells Greer. "I'm writing you a script for epinephrine. Keep it with you at all times. No more beekeeping without full protective gear."

Greer doesn't even nod. She keeps her eyes on her lap, grating the skin on her thumbs away like sheet a of sandpaper, unable to look at anyone. When I tried to sit at the edge of her hospital bed and coax her eyes to mine, she cast them away. So my ass is riding another uncomfortable chair. Meanwhile, Karen hovers by Greer's bedside, agreeing to everything the doctor is saying.

"Is she a candidate for venom immunotherapy? Mac had the shots after he was stung by multiple bees and swelled up."

"If Greer wants a referral, she can request it from her primary care." The physician shrugs off Karen's mothering.

"I'll just avoid the whole thing, thanks." Greer pipes up.

Based on the blank expression on her face, she means

all of it; immunotherapy, the prescription the doctor offers, the hives, the bees, and everything else that makes her happy.

When the doctor is done giving Greer advice on taking it easy over the next twenty-four hours, it's Mac who yanks the curtain around the metal track, closing the four of us off from the rest of the emergency room. He's read her apprehension correctly too.

He places a hand over the thin sheet, atop her knee. "We'll get you what you need. Take the rest of the week off. You'll probably feel worse later if your stomach troubles keep up."

Greer vomited in the ambulance.

"You too," he says, retracing his comforting palm in an about-face. "I don't suspect you'll want to leave Greer anyway, so you're off tomorrow as well."

"She should come home with us." Karen insists, brushing Greer's limp blonde hair off of her shoulder. "Reconsider, sweetheart. We have plenty of room."

"Karen, don't." Her husband responds to her aggressiveness. "I know you think you're helping, but Greer will be more comfortable at Byron's with her things."

The light in Karen's effectual smile fades. Bringing Greer home from the hospital was the first step toward getting Greer to move.

The nurse brings in discharge papers. Greer can get dressed. Karen wants to help, but Mac is firm when he says it is time for them to go. He wants to check the hives. Karen stubbornly disagrees. She plants herself like a tree. Forgetting my presence is of any consequence, she doesn't agree to leave until she's persuaded Greer to call if she needs anything. Then she repeats a reminder to Greer that she'll be over in the morning.

Our ride home is silent. Though not as unsteady on her feet as I would've anticipated, there's a precariousness to Greer. She's slow getting out of the car and taking those first few tentative steps to our front door. I prop her up under my arm, my palm attached to her waist, and walk with her to her room. Mac's input that Greer needs to be surrounded by familiarity guides my actions, pulling back the covers and tucking Greer into her bed.

I plan to be gone no longer than it takes for me to find a clean shirt, wash the grass and grit off my forearms, and get her a glass of water. Returning to Greer's room in under three minutes, I find she's up, stuffing clothes into a duffle. It's pink with worn appliquéd bows and hearts that are cracked and lifting. I saw the bag when Greer moved in, but how did I not notice it resembled what a child would pack in for a slumber party?

"What are you doing?" I still her hands as she shoves a stack of clothes from her drawer into the last open cranny. There is no way the bag is zipping shut.

"I shouldn't be here!" she yells, her voice still raspy from her throat constricting.

I huff, mocking Karen for the thought she's put in the forefront of Greer's mind. "Why not?"

"I made a mistake."

"Uh-huh. People do that. They make honest mistakes." I turn her chin so that Greer looks at me. So that she sees how relieved I am that she's okay and she hears much I love her without having to utter the words she's felt inadequate for not being able to say back.

This is a woman who split a hive, moved it three miles away, and waited to return to the original because Mac had warned her there was a possibility the bees might recognize her scent and find it threatening. She and Mac struck a deal to inspect their handiwork together, but Greer's drawn to those frightening little insects. For as freaked out as I am about her safety, as much as my throat closed up, my nose ran, and my eyes watered waiting for Greer to breathe after Mac slammed that fucking honking needle into her thigh, I wouldn't do anything other than encourage her to keep seeking out happiness.

It is badass.

"I should've known better. It was stupid not to ask Mac to come out there with me."

"And?" I nudge, understanding Mac was hot on her heels because he'd told me he was as excited to check out the progress as Greer was. Mac wasn't stopping Greer. He was joining her.

"It makes me feel insignificant and naive."

"And?"

"And I don't deserve—" She crumbles. My palms fit our waists closer together and she reaches up, holding on for dear life. Her short nails seek purchase in the hair at the nape of my neck. Her tears soak the shirt I've changed into. I'm glad it's clean, even if it won't be for long.

I tuck my nose, kissing the top of her head. "You don't want to go, honey bee. And I don't want you to go either. But you don't belong here."

Greer

The knife I'd thought cut my leg after being stung plunges into my gut. Sobs bleed out of me hearing I don't belong. There is nowhere for me. No good place to put a woman who made a life-altering decision before she grew up. No home for her to cultivate. No significant spot to find her bearings and make more of herself.

My legs give out, unable to carry the weight anymore. Byron catches me under the knees. I bury my face in his chest, pressing my eyes closed, trying to stop the falling tears. In his arms, I'm surrounded by warmth and a love I never expected would happen for me. I don't want to let go. This can't be ending.

I feel us moving through the house. If I were a small animal, I'd scramble over his shoulder to get away from the inevitable. I don't want to be set on the doorstep and sent on my way. I don't want to risk blinking and opening my eyes to the cruel reality that I'm better off gone from here. Away from Byron and every good thing he's brought into my life over the past months.

The next thing I know, softness meets my curved spine. A pillow beckons my tense muscles to relax. His scent surrounds me.

"That's better." Byron soothes.

His thumb caresses my jaw and my cheek nestles into his palm. The kisses he places at the corners of my eyelids have my will cracking. I want to see him. If only during these fleeting moments I want to watch the display of love he shows me. I finally get the nerve to look.

"Why are we in your bedroom?" Crying has done nothing to lessen the cracking in my raspy voice.

I reach out to touch him and Byron turns my hand, pressing the pads of my fingers to his mouth.

"Because, I almost lost you, Greer. And if forever with you only lasts another day, or a week—or I'm lucky enough to get years—from now on, I intend on falling asleep with you here in my bed. I want you to wake up feeling like the woman you are and not the child you're trapped pretending to be for the sake of others. I think we deserve to move on together from the ghosts that haunt our dreams instead of being separated by a stupid wall or the expectations people put on us. I want to die as happy a man as those bees make you, knowing I got to love you as long as you'll let me have you."

Byron's words wash over me, bringing a sense of calm to the room. It is in direct opposition to the turbulent whooshing as my blood pumps through my veins.

Passing out from the bee sting brought on a complete lack of control. The only thing that could fill the holes of uncertainty was the clawing need I had for comfort. But I hadn't wanted to admit how badly I carved Byron. I knew Mac and Karen stayed at the emergency room out of sincere concern for my welfare. I couldn't send them away and it felt lewd and arrogant flaunting our familiarity in front of anyone. So, to combat the desire for intimacy, I clenched my fists and refused to meet his concerned expression.

As if Byron truly understands my frailty, he hasn't let me go since we laid down in his room. Yet as I trace the collar of his tear-stained t-shirt, I concede not an ounce of that longing hasn't left. It's increased. And I'm hanging on the precipice of another cliffside and the chasm I had little reason to believe I'd ever cross.

"Do you want to stay here?" he asks while I'm searching for the nerve to reply.

"Yes." I nod. My eyes water and the image of his chest becomes fuzzy. I clutch his shirt.

"Okay." He sighs, pressing for an honest answer. "Tell me why being here is right for you."

Because I feel like a whole person when I'm with you. That there's hope for tomorrow. Because I don't want to let someone go who I care about the way I had to do the other times. "Because you accept me for who I am, and all my broken pieces fit back where they belong when we're together. Because I'm grateful for the way you love me, Byron, and how when you aren't even near, it still makes me feel like I'm more than I am." My face flames, when my voice cracks, admitting, "I love you."

Byron presses his mouth to mine. Our lips part in unison and I sweep my tongue inside, tasting the sweetness life has to offer me. He groans, rolling on top of me. My hands tear at the hem of his shirt, and he reaches back to pull it over his head. I shimmy my top off. Flicking the clasp of my bra, my breasts tumble unbound and Byron takes one in his mouth. His teeth graze over my nipple and he sucks the sting away and then moves on to the second to do the same while rocking his pelvis into mine.

My fingers thread through his hair, holding him to my tit, and I choke out, "I want you, Byron. I want this."

I've almost asked him to make love to me before, but I've lost the nerve. Tonight I don't want to panic, or worry the disconnect between my heart and my head— when I've dreaded Byron would make a big deal out of him being the first man inside of me, or worse, tell me no—is insurmountable.

He stops, tipping his chin toward me, his eyes dark with desire.

My face must betray my underlying thoughts, because Byron doesn't question if I'm sure. He doesn't say he's fine continuing to wait. I'm not waiting anymore. I've asked us to be patient about this long enough. I don't want to discuss anything or rehash the list of regrets I might feel afterward. I do few things on my terms, and this is one that I hold the position of power on. I won't fight the turbulent emotions about finally having sex, wondering what it feels like to surrender the last bastion. Byron will love me in the morning. I know he will.

Chapter Eighteen

Byron

I remove Greer's bottoms and shuck my own. Exactly zero about what we've ever done in bed has been chaste. Our self-restraint, *my self-restraint*, has only denied us the last act. This moment is important for Greer. Yet she's the same woman who doesn't want to be handled with kid gloves. She's ready to make this choice. Given that Greer plays with her pussy for me, and that she'll hold my fingers deep in her cunt when I use them to penetrate her, telling her I'll go slow or that I'll do my best so her first time isn't painful seems inane. I'd never hurt her.

I hook one of her legs over my elbow. Her other splays, her thigh falling to the side. She opens wide for me with the faintest coy smile playing on her lips. She's confident in the decision she's making, though her cheeks flush with anticipation. Spread out in my bed, her pussy glistens, pink and swollen. If I thought for a second she'd let me, I'd shimmy down her body, lick the sweetness from her folds, and make her toes curl. I'd like to hear my name fall from her lips and for her to beg me to fuck her, but there will be other times.

Stifling the thought that I should ask her if she wants me to put on a condom, I remember we're together. Tonight, tomorrow, for as long as Greer will have me. I'm hers and she's mine. We've laid our souls bare. I'll take everything that comes along with taking her skin to skin. The unknowns aren't really all that mysterious to an almost forty-year-old guy, are they? And the trust she's putting in me—the confidence she has that I'm honorable and would never intentionally hurt her— makes me believe I am a decent man.

Greer's eyelashes flutter as I slide the tip of my dick against her slit. Her breath comes in pants. Her breasts jiggle as her chest rises and falls. She's so beautiful and I can't believe she's giving herself to me.

I hold her leg underneath the knee and lean in, notching my cock into her channel. The short swift thrusts make Greer mewl. The tiny cries I know by heart from when I've worked her over. Her pussy quakes with soft ripples that grip me.

Resting my weight on one shoulder, I groan. "You feel so fucking perfect squeezing me already, honey bee," I whisper in her ear before kissing her.

She's been so wet whenever we've been intimate I'll have Greer milking my cock in no time. Just the thought of getting her off has my balls tightening.

Her hands are everywhere on my body, sliding down my biceps and up over the ridges in my back. Her fingers tangle in my hair, sucking my tongue into her mouth with drunken passion. I love that she's not holding back. That she loves this one last step we're taking. That's she was ready to share her body with me fully. That Greer is mine, and that I'm hers.

I press in harder, rotating my hips and grinding the base of my cock against her clit. At the conclusion and beginning of each consecutive circle, Greer whimpers. Her fingers knead into my ass, drawing me closer if I put a fraction of an inch of space between our torsos.

She kisses me like she can't get enough, and I devour her lips in kind as her touch becomes staccato, pinching and grabbing my skin, chasing the blissful high.

Her hips meet every motion, spurring me on, showing me what she likes. She's so close.

"Byron!" Greer cries. Her voice hitches as her body tenses. Her nails dig into my shoulder blades. She peaks and I ride her climax, praying I won't give into her orgasm without giving Greer a little more of the gratification she deserves.

Once she's found purchase, her hands gravitating downward to my ass, I push back on my knees and flip her leg over my head. She's even tighter in this position, with the flesh between her knees swollen. I bind her slender ankles with a fist, grunting and rutting. Greer's back arches. She flattens a single palm against the headboard. The other hand still digs in, guiding my thrusts, ensuring she's enjoying this.

I grit my teeth, able to tell when I hit the spot that drives her wild. Pleasure and pain are spelled out on Greer's face. It's the look of ecstasy and my ego is at an all-time high because I'm the one she wants putting it there.

My hips snap back and forth, harder, faster. She expels a flurry of dirty words before saying, "Please come. Please, make me come again. I need to feel it. I need to feel you."

Her pleading is all it takes for me to crash over the edge. I slam home, using my forearms to brace myself over her, hoping the force of spilling inside of Greer sets off her second orgasm. I'm rewarded with a deep, pulsing quiver that sucks my remaining energy dry and fills me up like nothing else ever has.

I hang over Greer. Her eyes are closed. The coy smile she wore before has morphed into something lazier, yet seemingly as self-assured. Though I could endlessly watch her relaxed and satiated expression, I pull out. In a fluid motion, Greer turns toward me as I gather her up in my arms.

I kiss her sweaty forehead. "How do you feel?" I ask with a "was it okay" inflection.

I'm not worried Greer didn't like it. But I'm not as cocky a bastard to assume my performance was perfect, or that Greer might not need reassurance that I'm here to talk out whatever she's feeling.

Greer

I snuggle under Byron's arm. My mouth opens and closes. Trying to find the right words.

A part of me—a big part of me that I've always psychologically battled with over never just "giving it up" to a male lover—is having her "I told you so" moment. However, that doesn't mean she was right. I'm glad it was Byron. That we shared our bodies the way we had before we shared *all* of us with the other person. And that the things we learned the other liked while spending nights together in my bed led the experience in his to be everything I wanted it to be.

Let's be honest, I wasn't exactly a purist before we had sex. I've never been shy about touching myself, not even in front of him. Byron's brought me to orgasm, leaving my thighs drenched when I come on many occasions. The worst idea of losing my virginity would've been him treating me like a delicate flower when he's stretched and fondled me and found out for himself what makes my entire body blush—and I don't mean from embarrassment.

I measure what I have to say and then go for broke, having faith he'll understand. "It was familiar and, at the same time, so different."

"That's definitely a good way to put it." He huffs a little laugh. "Are you sore?"

"No. I'm—I'm wet?" the pitch of my voice rises and I shift on the mattress. "I think I'm laying in a puddle."

My quip has Byron full-on laughing. "If you want me to use something next time, condoms make clean up less messy. Well, at least for you it would." He trails a finger down my collar bone. Circling my breast, he encases it with his palm and tweaks my nipple. "Need to suck on this." Byron ducks his head. The pull of his mouth reaches between my legs, but I can't let go of his last comment.

"Is that what we should be doing? Do you want me to see a doctor?" I haven't got the foggiest when it comes to birth control. Safe sex is... It's this, right? Waiting for the person who completes you and trusting you're both doing the correct thing?

His eyes flick to mine, and Byron flattens me to the mattress. He spreads his palm wide over my belly. "I told you I'm taking as many days as forever lasts with you, Greer. I want you to read between the lines on that, and for you to understand whatever happens, happens. There is no way of knowing what tomorrow has in store, but it's going to take a lot to tear me away from you. I seriously have no plans to go anywhere—not without you by my side. Okay?"

"Okay." My lips twist. I try to spin, angling away from him to conceal my glee.

"What?" Byron catches my waist. His chest hair scratches my back and his fingertips tickle my sides. I roll to my stomach, relieving the tingling sensation. Byron's hard cock slides between my butt cheeks, slipping toward my pussy, and rousing another as I shimmy my hips up.

"If you love me and I love you, uhm—Do you possibly want to bury your hatchet inside of me again?"

I may not have been sore after the first time or even the second, but by the next morning, I may have *juuuust* a tad overestimated what my body could handle. I'm positive while letting the hot water run over me in the shower the next morning that the person who came up with the saying "too much of a good thing" was talking about sex.

Dressed in comfy clothes and drying my hair with a towel, I pad into the kitchen.

"Good thing we're staying home today. You're walking a little ginger there, honey bee." Byron waggles his brows, reaching out to draw me into his arms. He kisses me softly. "I'll go easier on you tonight. And," he tacks on, "maybe give you a ride to work next week. Unless you want driving lessons?"

I stiffen and pull away. "No, thanks."

"Woah, Woah! What did I say?"

"I thought I made it clear I'm not interested in driving."

"You did." He runs a hand over his scalp. His shoulders shrink, and he sighs, shaking his head. "I'm sorry. You have every right to change your mind, or not to."

"What's that supposed to mean?" I spit.

Byron's lips purse. He heaves a breath. "You have this line drawn about not getting your license again. You're worried you'll hurt someone. Fine. I respect it. But why can't you draw a line with Karen? Why do you let her continually drag you back and allow her to hurt you?"

The doorbell rings before I can retort. Of course, it is Karen interrupting. What else would intrude on a fight besides my past, especially since it's the impetus of most of our disagreements?

Karen perches on the sofa, clutching my hand, and looking grave as she asks how I'm feeling. I tell her I'm fine out of reflex, Byron's accusation ringing in my ears.

"Mac and I had an argument on the way home from the hospital." Karen swallows. "He accused me of holding on too tight. Holding you back. I told him he was a fool until he pushed about stopping to check the hives and made me face why it bothered me. The reality is, Mac didn't want me to agree. He wanted me to tell him that those bees were *his* thing. What he's cared for since Ellis has been gone. I was caring for *you*. And he replied, 'Then why is Greer out there with me?'." She tilts her chin to Byron, who is blending in against the wall. "I understand why you both avoid me. Now, more than ever."

"I love you, Karen." I pause, understanding Byron and Mac are right. They've both paved the road for this discussion. "But I'm not the person I was. I'm not even the girl Ellis grew up with anymore, and I only remember so many stories about who we were."

"I don't like bees." She graces me with a watery smile and a silly eye roll. "But the soaps you make are lovely, and I'd like you to teach me how to make them. I can come here if it's easier for you. I'd like to learn the process, and maybe in the process, get to know the you who Mac's so keen to see succeed."

One year later...

"Put the broom down," Karen huffs, holding a ream of shiny paper to her chest. "Ester will be here in twenty. That's her job."

"Force of habit," I reply. Unapologetically, I toss my chin toward an open box and a baker's dozen of rose and cedar beard oil. "I ran out of labels and needed to stay busy while you were at the print shop."

Karen sets the stickers atop the boxes that are set to ship. She lifts a bottle off of the counter while I make a tidy dust pile in the corner. It is part of Ester's job, but I don't mind pitching in. Someone else helped me once upon a time, too.

Together, Karen and I affix the last of the labels on our latest product. I use the big fancy tape dispenser that makes the ripping and squealing sound to seal it shut. Karen pats the stack of boxes. "I can't believe how popular this scent is. I get daily emails asking if we'll make candles and lotion with the same scent."

There's an ease to my conversations with Ellis's mom nowadays. It started the first afternoon we melted wax in my haphazard double boiler. Having a task to keep us occupied made learning about who the other person was fun.

Come to find out Karen's hatred of bees is as minute as the tip of their stingers. Initially, we spent one week a month goofing off in the kitchen. After those four weeks, we had an insane amount of product—way more than the random orders the mill girls had requested. Karen suggested renting a booth at the Farmer's Market.

There was a flurry of activity and interest at our tables. We were a buzz when it happened; A Brighton townie who had been circling the tent we were under, pointed at me saying, "Aren't you?"

They glanced in Karen's direction. The stiff movement of their arm followed their jaw-dropping gaze. The gall of the next question took Karen by surprise. Her eyes widened with the same shock as the customer's had, and it was obvious Karen hadn't clued in that I was still recognized for what I did.

My heart sank, trying to come up with a way to assuage the situation. As I opened my mouth, Karen beat me to responding.

"Oh, mind your own beeswax," she trilled in that lovely southern *bless your heart* manner.

And the customer, who hadn't intended on buying anything anyway, moved on to the next booth.

I blew out a breath and Karen hugged me from the side, making sure everyone saw. We ended the day on a happier note. Everything we'd brought had sold out.

So we made more, and when it came time to package our wares up, Karen presented me with a bundle of labels that read: Mind Your Own Beeswax, LLC. It wasn't as if we weren't going to have to deal with people's perceptions and opinions, so we might as well set the tone.   The next month we returned to the market with a website and a slightly more professional flair.

Almost immediately, we didn't have enough time or inventory to keep up with the demand. Eight months ago, we'd made a huge dent in the decade of beeswax Mac had stored. Six months ago, my best friend's parents cashed out his college fund. Mine offered the equivalent of mine, which they'd had to take the loss on anyhow when things had gotten rough for my dad. My mom drove to Brighton before Thanksgiving, when we were swamped with gift orders. However, it hadn't taken much for Karen to agree to me talking to Phil to find someone who needed a lift the way I had. He recommended Ester. Aside from keeping us tidy, she's the extra set of hands we often need when we're at our busiest.

Mother's Day is around the corner and we fully expect to get slammed.

I place my hand over my stomach and then scoot my crossed arms up, smashing my cleavage together. It doesn't help my sore boobs.

"You look pensive. Are you okay, Greer?"

"Oh, yeah," I wave Karen off. "I just remembered Paisley's inventory list is somewhere around here." I twist my hips. A crooked smile plays on my lips.

Karen grins right back and pats me on my arm. By this time next year, we may even have a storefront in downtown Brighton. "I have it in my car along with the rest of her monthly order. Do you want to double-check it, or add some samples?"

"Yes, please. If you don't mind. All I need is the printout to match up with last month's. I don't want to give Paisley anything extra that she's not selling out of or samples that her customers won't like." Word of mouth through the boutique has been stellar.

When Karen leaves, I take a deep breath. I'm honest about my relationship with Byron. Karen knows how serious we are. Yet it's nice to keep our secrets to ourselves.

Not disappointed in the least by our luck, Byron and I avoided the inevitable for months. Then the business boomed, and we decided on the rhythm method. Except, the person who came up with that brilliant idea was truly clueless. No sex when I'm at my horniest is a recipe for disaster. We did so well through the holiday rush. Those days were sort of like what it was like when we were first exploring what we meant to one another.

But I caved so hard… so, so hard last month.

The way my body feels right now, it could go either way. And this is the first time I might actually be disappointed that I'm not pregnant and maybe Byron and I do have to have *the talk* to see if we're going to start trying instead of leaving it up to chance. But I'm certain that either way, he'll be with me each step of the way.

Thank you for reading Deep Gap! I hope you enjoyed Greer and Byron's deeply emotional love story as much as I loved writing about them.

What will an obsessive alpha like Jake Ballentine risk to stay in control? Enjoy this preview of **Bleeding Heart**, a runaway bride, enemies to lovers romance!

BLEEDING HEART

Paisley

"Paisley, will you have Gavin as your lawfully wedded husband, to live together in the covenant of matrimony? Will you love him, comfort him, honor and keep him, in sickness and in health, and forsaking all others, keep you only unto him, for the rest of your life?"

The end of the minister's sentence fades, overcome by the loud whooshing in my ears. Sweat that has already dampened the satin at my armpits and down the back of my gown, making the soft fabric itchy and uncomfortable, now trickles between my breasts. My breaths come in short pants. My heart, searching for escape, is threatening to beat outside of my chest. Not literally, though once a man like Gavin held it cradled in their hands as gently as my husband-to-be is holding my hands.

My tongue darts to wet my parched lip. The underside gets caught on the smudge-proof lipstick the makeup artist applied. We've spared no expense for this wedding. I'd seen candelabras. Gavin suggested the ceremony be at night. And the chapel is lit by candlelight! We are what everyone deems perfect for one another.

Gavin loves me. I love him. How could I not? He's a good man.

But do I not honor Gavin and devalue our relationship by continuing with this wedding? Or do I love him enough to be the "anyone who knows a reason" why we shouldn't marry one another?

keep you only unto him

for the rest of your life

I'd abide by those words if somewhere deep in my gut my shriveling soul was interpreting them the same way that Gavin is.

That's what I have.

A black soul for playing along with a lie until it was too late and embarrassing Gavin in public.

We're in a church, for Christ's sake!

Oh, crap. If I weren't spinning the wheel trying to decide which path to hell the arrow will point me in, then taking Lord's name in vain has added a short, direct route.

Lightheaded, I wrap my left hand over my stomach and bend at the waist. Gavin's thumb presses into the top of my left hand. His fingers pinch into my palm.

"Paisley, are you okay?" His voice filled with concern, Gavin shifts his stance so that he's shielding me from the pews occupied by our family and Gavin's friends and colleagues from the hospital.

"Just, *ah*, give me a sec." The sheer fabric of my veil flops over my shoulder, covering my watery eyes. I try some deep breathing exercises. My chest aches. My fingertips are cold and tingling. Perspiration drenches my scalp.

My mother's compliment from before she escorted me down the aisle rushes at me like a tidal wave. *You're going to have the most beautiful marriage, Paisley. I'm so happy you found a man that loves you unconditionally and that you have a bright beginning, similar to what your father and I had.*

I wanted to tell my mom that Gavin's love comes with strings attached. That he couldn't keep me only unto him, no matter how short our life together winds up being. Gavin needs more.

I can't live trapped in the cage of domestic bliss. I don't want him to kiss me goodbye in the morning and drive away in his BMW, pretending I'm the woman he still wants.

Both of us can't lie.

I can't marry Gavin.

And now that I've made up my mind, I'm in a huge pickle, aren't I?

"Oh, gosh!" I whip my head back, standing ramrod straight. I brush away the layers of tulle resting on my head to get them out of my face. When that doesn't work, I grip the tiny pearl and silver tiara from Sterlings that the veil is attached to and rip it entirely out of my hair. Giving Gavin a wide-eyed and wily smile, I'm positive he's ready to have me committed to the psychiatric wing.

"Sweetheart?" Gavin's gaze is wrought with concern.

"You are going to make an amazing husband." I pat underneath the knot in his silk cravat. "But you shouldn't waste the happiness the world has to offer you on me."

I turn toward the chancel and bolt. My skirt swishes

past the altar and I duck out the door in front of the minister's vestry. The corridor leads to the stairs, to the lower floor where I waited to march down the aisle, and outside to the parking lot.

"Paisley!" Gavin yells.

I doubt he'll stay put. I mean, would any groom if they were questioning why their bride left them at the altar? But I don't have an answer Gavin will accept. He'll coerce me back inside and I'll give in so as not to disappoint anyone.

The streetlights above light up the sky the moment I step outside. It casts a glow over the rows of parked cars, highlighting that none are of any use without a set of keys. The limo driver, charged with whisking the new Dr. and Mrs. Gavin Laughton to the reception, is waiting at the entrance of the church. Quickly, I realize I've skipped from one problem to the next. I need to find my way out of here.

"This is why robbers don't wait until the last minute to figure out their getaway plan, Paisley!" I chastise myself aloud.

I lift my gown off the blacktop, ball it in my fists, and start running. My high heels pinch my toes when my feet land on the pavement, making my lips twist. *Shoot!* I was sorely mistaken thinking the blisters I'd have by the end of tonight would be from dancing the night away.

I stop, hop up and down, remove my shoes, and let them clop to the ground. A twinge of guilt hits me. They were such nice shoes. It's followed by a second pang of regret. How can I be sad about ditching Jimmy Choos when I just left the man I was supposed to marry in the most compromising position anyone could find themselves in?

Well, maybe it's not *the* most. But getting ditched ranks up there for embarrassment. Poor Gavin. And my poor mother... *Eeeh.* My mother. I'll find a way to live this fiasco down, but can they?

"Paisley? Where are you?"

"Oh shit, he's still after me!" I squeak.

Skittering onto the cold and damp sidewalk, I pick up the pace. Within the next few blocks, I'm going to go from Historic Brighton to Downtown Brighton to the back alleyways that investment firms thought twice about revitalizing.

Beyond a chain link fence, flashing pink letters on a neon sign catch my attention. Almost out of breath from the heavy layers I'm carrying, I have two choices. I can keep running and risk the possibility of getting hepatitis when I step on a needle. Or I can duck inside and pray that Sweet Caroline's is the last place on earth anyone—especially a well-respected heart surgeon—will come looking for me.

There's a single car in the lot, so I take my chances that the customers won't think I'm part of the stage show. I scoot under an awning, ignoring the marquee advertising the scantily clad headline acts, and pull on a door handle.

"No, no. Don't be locked. Don't be locked!" I dare to glance over my shoulder, reaching for the other door.

Not as heavy as I expect, it swings open, nearly toppling me over. I step into the dark strip club, pulling my dress inside before I can't see anything anymore, and risk it catching between the doors. My practically bare feet can feel the holes in my stockings and the short pile of the rug.

"We're closed," booms a voice from down a dark hall.

"I need to use the phone. Make a call." I arch my spine six ways from Sunday, trying to see in the shadows.

I'm also wondering who exactly am I calling? And how am I paying for the lift because my purse, with my phone and my credit cards, are in the church's undercroft.

Thank fuck I own a boutique because not making off with the money would make bank robbery an exceptionally poor career choice.

A tall silhouette emerges, back lit by the hallway. He uses the top of a liquor bottle to flip a switch, washing the entire theater in harsh light. I cover my eyes for them to adjust.

"Don't you have a cell?" The man demands, accusing me of being an idiot.

A whole congregation agrees you're not far off, dude.

"I lost it." Along with my sanity.

I blink, and the man across the room is staring at me in shock.

Can't say I blame him. I'm sort of shocked about how my night is going, too. Although, I'm the slightest bit more prepared for this encounter than Sweet Caroline's proprietor is.

From the looks of the desolate parking lot, I thought there would be a bartender in here. A bouncer. A regular watching a dancer spin around a pole, too enamored by the woman taking her clothes off on stage to become involved in my little circus act. After humiliating myself in front of two hundred people who I know, what difference would half a dozen who I don't make?

However, I hadn't factored Jake Ballentine into the mix.

No downtown business owner has to have met him to know him. Jake is a man whose reputation precedes him. His omnipotent presence in this small town is as much an institution as the gentleman's club he owns.

More than Jake's questionable dealings tower above. From across the room, he looms gigantic. Long and lean, Jake is dressed in crisp black trousers. His unbuckled belt jangles at his hips. Several buttons on his shirt are undone at the collar. The power in his neck and broad shoulders is similar to a competitive swimmer. His tie hangs loose. His blond hair is disheveled like he's gripped it at the root, but it appears he's also tried to mat it down and back into place.

I'm uncertain if the attempt to make himself look presentable is for my benefit. I would have buckled the belt first, but that's just me, and I'm a girl.

Jake strides over the carpeting with the bottle of amber liquid in his grip. He sets it on a small round table as he passes.

"I thought the princess lost a shoe leaving the ball?"

I crane my neck to reply. "Oh, I did that bitch one better." I lift the tattered hem of my soiled gown and wiggle my toes.

His cantankerous laughter bounces off the walls. "Come on, which one of the guys set me up?" He shakes his head, unbelieving. "I could have sworn Trig and Carver were having too much fun with their respective wives to notice I left."

I shake my head in response. "No clue what you are talking about. Didn't know you were closed. Didn't remember my cell."

Jake plays with the cleft in his square chin. His pupils are wide and black with an icy blue halo. He stares, daring me to hide the truth from him. "It can't be that simple."

"Uh, yeah. It can," I say sarcastically. It is the truth and I'm coming down from the adrenaline high of hot-footing it out of a church during my wedding. "So can I —"

The door flings open interrupting me.

"I need to use your phone. Please! I left mine at the church a few blocks away and I need to tell my fiancée's mother… Paisley?"

Oh, fuckkity, fuck, fuck.

My shoulders hit my ears. I'm caught in Jake's blue-eyed tractor beam, unable to turn and look at Gavin.

"Just go with it," I whisper under my breath.

I jump before even realizing what I'm doing. Wrapping my arms around his neck, the Norse God's palms encase my ass, and our bodies press flush together. Jake plays along, kissing me as if runaway brides barrel into his establishment every single day, searching for sanctuary.

And while this kiss isn't the one I anticipated ending my wedding day with, I have to admit Jake Ballentine is an amazing kisser.

Ready to read more?
Bleeding Heart is available now!
www.jodykaye.com/bleedingheart

To view more great titles, sign up for Jody Kaye's newsletter, or find her on social media go to www.jodykaye.com or

Scan Now!

About the Author

Jody's husband asked what she'd been doing all day. After five years she finally confessed, "When no one is around, I write."

Okay, it was more like a bunch of stammering and trying to get out of saying a thing. Jody's a writer. You want it pretty. Let's compromise.

"Just finish one," he said, challenging her to complete a story and share it. Little did he know that those words of encouragement meant they'd return from a family vacation with a wild and defiant set of quintuplets stumbling their way into adulthood. Wasn't raising their three sons enough?

A native of nowhere, Jody settled in New England for 17 years before agreeing to uproot her brood of boys and move to North Carolina. She's a part-time graphic designer and marketeer with over twenty years' experience, and full-time writer. If Jody ever gets lost, you'll find her reading, all the while hoping that her ravenous children haven't eaten all the ingredients before she's cooked dinner.

**Add your voice and help readers discover
this love story by writing a review!**